ATHENA'S
LEGACY

ATHENA'S LEGACY

A novel by

Robert Lee

ISBN-13: 978-0615965789
ISBN-10: 0615965784

LCCN: 2014932837

First Printing February 2014

G

Printed in the USA
G J Publishing
515 Cimarron Circle Suite 123
Loudon TN 37774
865-458-1355
www.neilans.com

ACKNOWLEDGMENT

I would be remiss if I did not mention the valuable assistance and advice given to me by my beloved Barbara. Her devotion to this writing endeavor never wavered, and she gave me steady encouragement. I could not have completed this novel without her help. Thanks, Barbara.

INTRODUCTION

In today's world we see many occurrences that are strange and not easily explained. Such was the situation with Jeff Benson who could not realize how a visit to the Parthenon in Nashville, Tennessee in his youth would have far reaching implications later in life. The encounter there with the statue of the Greek goddess Athena was exhilarating but seemed of no consequence until years later, when her spirit moved into his life, and Jeff saw Athena's image in his own love affair. Soon members of his inner circle were also affected, succumbing to her supernatural mysticism.

How could such an inanimate structure of ivory and gold exert influence over Jeff and others just as she had done in ancient Greece?

In Homer's Iliad, Athena, the goddess of wisdom and war, was widely worshipped in ancient Greece, and her likeness was found in recessed sanctuaries in homes and palaces throughout the country. Bold and beautiful in appearance, and forty-two feet tall, her statue anchored one end of the Parthenon.

Athena's ability to inspire is depicted through lore and epic writings. She fought alongside warriors using Zeus's thunderbolt. When Achaean was wounded in battle, she guided his spear, a symbol of prowess.

Athena could, at times of her choosing, assume human characteristics. In one well known myth, the mortal Arachne, a student of Athena, was renowned for her mastery in weaving. In a feeling of competitiveness, she dared Athena to a contest of their skills. Athena, jealous and furious with Arachne's arrogance, changed her into a spider and condemned her to spin and draw silk from her own body for all time.

Greeks knew the fable of how the builder Mnesicles, while constructing a temple, slipped from a great height. With no hope for his recovery, the doctor Pericles allowed the goddess Athena to cure him. This led to the erection of a gold structure of her that became known as Athena Hygenia.

Athena felt Jeff Benson's awe-struck feelings toward her, but when she witnessed Jeff's love affair with Barbara Douglas, the spurned Athena unleashed the full brunt of her jealous rage.

Marcia Leed, trusting and perhaps naive, never realized some kind of outside force was upon her until too late. Would this form of curse to her marriage culminate as a blessing in disguise?

Clara Bowman, a vixen, with scruples no match for her driving ambition, appeared to embrace some of Athena's psyche. Athena saw herself in Clara and apparently entered into Clara's soul.

Is it possible the same goddess who fought alongside warriors in the Trojan wars would be capable of causing an unmitigated death?

Finally, Athena atones for her misdeeds by curing a most unusual ailment in a most unusual way.

PART ONE

CHAPTER ONE

Jeffrey Benson opened his mail, then rushed into his supervisor's office. Frank Vittori was on the phone. Jeff backed away and waited in the hallway.

"What's up, Jeff"

"The ASCE technical reports committee accepted our paper and invited Rex and me to deliver it at their next meeting."

Frank was pleased with the achievement of his favorite protégés, and quickly offered congratulations. He knew it was a special honor since Jeff and Rex Newton had been with the firm just over two years.

"I know you two worked hard and spent a lot of time and did a lot of research on that paper. Looks like it paid off. Costa Rica is a great place, too. I'll see how much we can help with expenses. I'll shoot for one hundred percent. Have you told Rex?"

"No, but I will right away."

Rex was busy with a client when Jeff found him, but he finished up quickly and turned to his colleague. "Hey, Jeff. You look especially happy this morning."

"Have I ever got good news for you!"

"Really? Is this a joke?"

"Far from it. Be thinking about a trip to San Jose, and I don't mean California."

Rex lit up. "How 'bout that! We did it." Then he extended his hand for a high five.

Their relationship had started when both were co-op students at the Pacific Institute of Technology; Jeff in Civil Engineering and Rex in Architecture. The arrangement consisted of a semester of classes followed by a semester of related work. After graduation both men accepted jobs with their work sponsor, Atlas Architects and Engineers. Over time they bonded into a strong friendship.

*****

After weeks of map reading and vacation guide studying, the friends boarded a Boeing 747 bound for Costa Rica. Jeff was seated in 18A and Rex was two rows back in the center section, so they found conversation between them difficult. After the flight had been underway for a couple of hours their talking had turned into shouting. The passenger next to Jeff, in 18B, offered to swap seats with Rex.

Jeff politely turned down the offer. "I see too much of my friend. It's good to be away from him for awhile."

Jeff walked to the rear of the plane to stand up and give himself a break from sitting. The lady from 18B made her way back a few minutes later, and asked, "Are you waiting for the restroom?"

"No, I just had to get on my feet."

After both had returned to their seats, the lady introduced herself. "I'm Mai Lois."

"I'm Jeff Benson. Pleased to meet you. Are you going to Costa Rica for the first time?"

"Yes. I hope to combine some pleasure with my business. Here's my business card."

The small card read:

Mai Lois McCoy
Travel Consultant
Worldwide Connections, Inc.
Pasadena, California 95113
1-888-555-7612
mlmccoy@live.com

"I never miss an opportunity to sell myself," she smiled.

*****

Jeff and Rex arrived at the Juan Santamaria International Airport about noon. After a hassle with immigration, they settled into their hotel, the El Pacifico.

"Are you ready for your presentation, Jeff?"

"I should be. I've been rehearsing it long enough."

That evening they walked the few blocks to the Grand Ambassador Hotel where their meeting was to be held. They arrived in time for Happy Hour, registered, picked up their name tags, and kibitzed with some of the other attendees.

Jeff was really nervous by the time he finally took his turn at the podium. His topic, "*Using Computer SketchUp Modeling to Design Solar Powered Buildings,*" was well received, however, and several attendees complimented him afterward.

*****

The next day Rex, hoping to land a big marlin, took a trip to Quepos, a small sport fishing town nearby. Rex went all out to be an outdoorsman. He did not have the physical qualities of an athlete with his five foot nine inch, slightly pudgy frame, and he never really tried to participate, much less excel, in sports. Fishing and hunting were his fortes.

Jeff, on the other hand, chose to take a tour of the city and nearby points of interest. When the tour van came to his hotel, he recognized a familiar face aboard – none other than that of Mai Lois.

"Well, fancy seeing you here," he shouted.

She responded more quietly, "You never know who you might see." She was outfitted in stretch capris and a hot pink tee. Her high wedgie style shoes added the height she needed; she was only about five foot three.

Jeff found her attractive, except for her closely cropped bleached hair. As they approached the first stop to view the Irazu Volcano, he followed behind her, watching her movements while trying not to stare. He reasoned that she was perhaps in her mid-thirties or early forties, but her shape and demeanor belied her age.

As they drew closer, they saw that fog surrounded the volcano crater, obstructing their view, but the smoke emitting from the core was visible.

Mai Lois began to take photos, moving closer to the edge.

"Will you take one of me here?"

"Sure. But don't get too close."

"Now I want to take a picture of you, Jeff."

The tour guide offered to take one of the two of them together. Mai Lois gave her instructions and handed her the camera.

When they were back in the van and headed for the coffee plantation, Jeff spoke. "This reminds me. I had the best coffee ever at breakfast this morning. Costa Rican coffee is the world's best – according to what I hear. Good food, too."

"I wish I could say the same. My breakfast at the Bonita Latino was just so-so, and dinner last night wasn't much better. Expensive, too."

"Why don't you come over to my hotel? You would have a choice of the buffet or ordering from the menu."

"That's something to think about."

The tour ended at noon. Jeff lunched alone, then decided to walk around and see the city unescorted. *What's happening? I'm breathing a heavy dose of exhaust fumes. Obviously catalytic converters are not required by law here.* Looking around, he saw that the stores were all locked up. *Siesta time. Not much to see now. Maybe the scenes will be better later.* The sight of large billboards with cigarette ads ruined an otherwise attractive landscape.

*****

When she returned to her room, Mai Lois viewed the pictures. She was especially pleased with the shots of Jeff. In his shorts, his trim body and athletic build looked great; and his six foot four frame set them off nicely. *Wait till I show these to the girls back at the office. Will they ever turn green with envy.*

*****

Jeff returned to his hotel about four o'clock and sat down to read some of the tourist pamphlets. He took off his shoes and plopped himself on the bed. He rolled over to face the telephone, musing: *Should I?* It didn't take him long to answer that question.

He dialed the front desk of the Bonita Latino and after finally getting through to the English speaking staff he obtained Mai Lois' number. "Hello, Mai Lois?"

(Pause.) "Yes?"

9

"This is Jeff. Hope I'm not intruding."

"No,"

"I'm wondering if you would join me for dinner here at my hotel."

(Pause.) "I would like that. I don't enjoy eating alone."

"Good. How's seven-ish sound?"

"Fine."

"I'll be waiting in the dining room."

*****

Unrestricted euphoria overcame Mai Lois. She tried but could not rein in the sudden outburst of excitement. Her grip on the telephone weakened, and it dropped to jiggle in the cradle before falling to the floor. *Oh my. Am I that nervous?* she wondered, as she grabbed the receiver to hang it up. *I wasn't sure Jeff would make good on his invitation, but here it is. And I'm so thrilled I can't think straight. That rich baritone voice ... how it makes me flutter!* To calm herself, she tried staring at the blank wall, but that was no help. *I'll look out the window; perhaps that will slow down my excitement.* The busy pedestrian traffic, however, didn't help. If anything, it made it worse.

Now what will I wear? She wondered, as she rummaged through her closet. *Why in God's name did I bring that low-cut dress that shows my cleavage? I'm so damn rattled. Hell, I'm acting like a deb just coming of age and going to a cotillion. Well, I am like that in a way – this will be my first date since Marvin passed on. Well, maybe this is not a bona fide date, but I'm damn sure treating it like one.*

*****

When Jeff saw her coming through the door into the dining room a few minutes after seven, she was in a classic wrap dress. The

10

pattern was flattering, as was the soft coral shade, complimented with jewelry, heels, the works.

He felt obliged to tell her she was well-dressed, not realizing his personal attention made her feel a bit uncomfortable.

She directed the conversation away from herself. "How was your afternoon?"

"Fine. I hope to see more of the country tomorrow. I'm scheduled to visit the rain forest."

"Me too. I'll be on the same tour, I think."

Jeff asked the waiter about the vintage wines, then settled for a bottle of Kendall Jackson cabernet. They decided to order their dinners from the menu.

Because this was her first visit to the area, Mai Lois wanted to focus on learning everything she could about it. "Nothing like first hand experience. Many of my clients are choosing Costa Rica, and some are even considering retiring here. There are many advantages, plus the people are friendly to Americans. What do you think about this country, Jeff?"

"I've been doing some reading. I didn't know this is a democratic country. No army, and no revolutions like so many other Latin American countries. It's so diverse, too. It's a microcosm of the United States. I read that its former President Oscar Arias Sanchez won a Nobel Peace Prize. I like it. It's beautiful, too. However, I would never live here.

"You wouldn't want to leave California?" asked Mai Lois.

"Not now."

"You're not likely a California native. What took you there in the first place?"

"I got a partial scholarship after high school to any college of my choosing. I grew up in a little town in Colorado – Carson Springs. My first thoughts were to attend a school in-state, but circumstances changed that and worked in my favor. My uncle ...

he was a manager at a plastics factory ... lived only two miles from Pacific Tech. When he found out about my interest in engineering, he urged me to attend college there and insisted that I stay with his family. Needless to say, that was a sweet deal, so I took him up on his offer. For a while, things worked out just fine ... delicious food and a short bike ride to classes. Then he was transferred back east. What a jarring blow for me. It meant I had to look at other options. I was lucky, and got accepted into the co-op program at Tech which really helped out with expenses – not to mention the work experience.

"I met Rex Newton, an architectural student, when we were assigned to the same project that year. We shared a room and did some of our own cooking. After graduation, we both decided to stay with the employer where we had done our co-op work. Rex now is not just a close friend; he's more like a brother. Now, enough about me. How about you and the travel business?"

"Well, I've been in it only about six months. I'm still learning, but I'm making expenses and putting some food on the table."

"How did you choose that line of work?"

"I needed additional income, plus I needed an outlet for my free time. I wasn't ready to retire."

"You're not old enough to retire."

"If you're fishing to find out my age, I'm not biting."

Mai Lois opened up about her own life. Her only business experience went back many years to her employment as secretary for a department head at the Allegheny Chemical Company in Pittsburg. Marvin, a PhD chemist from West Virginia University, took notice of her beauty. After a short romance they married and settled down to a happy and comfortable life. Several years later, Marvin transferred to a branch lab in Pasadena. Soon problems arose. He had never been active physically, but now he became sedentary. All he wanted to do was watch TV sports, eat, and drink beer. He followed the Pirates and Steelers as much as possible;

however, nearly any team would do. His health declined to the point that he was forced to take a disability retirement. On one particular occasion, which she remembered with painful detail, Mai Lois had prepared a healthy lo-cal dinner; but Marvin took one look at it, walked over to the telephone, and ordered a pizza.

"The day I had dreaded arrived. I returned from grocery shopping to find an ambulance parked in our driveway. As I moved closer I knew before I looked that Marvin was dead. One heart attack was all it took ... oh, it's getting late. I should be getting back to my hotel."

Jeff glanced at his watch. "It's after ten. *Tempus fugit.* Time really does fly when you're having a good time. It might not be safe out there. I'll walk you back."

"Oh, thank you, that'll be nice."

They headed down Playa deLeon, and could hear shouts of laughter and spirited singing from a cabaret across the wide expanse.

Jeff nodded his head in the direction of the noise. "I lost some sleep last night. These folks know how to party. I could hear their music well into the wee hours of the morning."

Soon Jeff and Mai Lois crossed a narrow street. It was so dark that footing required a gingerly placement of each step. It gave Jeff the opportunity to extend his hand like a true gentleman would. First, just a light grip, then he squeezed. Mai Lois responded with a smile. He felt more confident now that he had seen her display of approval, and assured himself that this was a "go" signal.

"I've liked you from the very beginning, Mai Lois. I'm glad we met."

Mai Lois was overjoyed at receiving Jeff's attention. She would have wanted her friends or at least an audience to see them together if it had been daylight. *Some ego boost, too. It's not every day you have an escort like this!*

At the end of the dark street they entered a wide boulevard with a small park in the center. The beauty was apparent even at night, with the full moon reflecting from the leaves on many of the plants. A jacaranda created a romantic setting with the moonbeams shining on its lavender blossoms.

Jeff wondered about the possible romance lying ahead. *I must be the only recent man in her life, the way she's acting,* he thought. He knew it would not be the beginning of anything remotely long-term since she was at least ten years his senior. That age differential, however, was certainly no deterrent to his strong desires.

They stopped to look around. Jeff removed his hand from hers, then grasped her waist to pull her closer. A light kiss on the back of her neck seemed to elicit a shiver of pleasure. When she turned around to face him directly, they embraced and kissed.

Mai Lois began to respond physically. *I feel an ache, but it is a pleasant ache. What's happening? Something is gushing inside my head. This is surreal.*

Jeff could tell from her facial expression and her rapid breathing that she was becoming excited. Hand in hand, they picked up the pace to her hotel.

When they reached the lobby, Jeff led her to the elevator, which took them to the sixth floor. As they reached the door to her room he said, "If we were in a movie scene, I would be invited in for a nightcap." She remained silent, but smiled as she unlocked the door.

Jeff laughed at his own quip. "I'm not wearing a cap; what do you think?"

She took his hand and led him toward the bedroom. He began smothering her with kisses. His arms entangled her small body. She started helping him with her undressing. He could see that her exposed body was free of blemishes, with not even a mole, not even the tiniest of vein marks. His thoughts were focused on the score, but looking at her, he wondered how anyone could ever choose food over this.

Then, as if some mechanical device had been triggered, she rose, pulled away, and shouted, "No! No! I can't go through with this."

Jeff, bewildered, asked, "What's the matter?"

"It's Marvin ... I'm still grieving over him. He's still on my mind."

Jeff turned away, asking himself, *Am I pissed? Hell yes, you bet I am!* He left, confused and disappointed.

*****

The next day the tour van pulled up to Jeff's hotel promptly at nine o'clock. Neither he nor Mai Lois exchanged greetings and did not speak to one another for the entire trip to the Veragua rain forest. They boarded the little tram and soon they were in the midst of a jungle, with the antics of monkeys and the chirping of birds all around them. A toucan with a rainbow beak lit on a branch above.

Mai Lois broke the silence, saying she was sorry and had not intended to lead him on.

Jeff replied, "I left your room angry, but soon understood your feelings. You must have had a great love for Marvin. Let me make a prediction, Mai Lois. Somehow, someday you will meet Mr. Right. He will help you overcome your bereavement and everything will be wonderful for you. Remember that."

"You're very noble."

CHAPTER TWO

Two years had elapsed since Jeff Benson and Rex Newton had returned from their trip to Costa Rica. Rex began taking weekend trips to San Diego to date a girl he had met at his high school reunion. Becky Timmons was rebounding from a nasty divorce. Her ex was one of those immature oafs who had left her with a mountain of debt and a bad credit rating. Only by her family's coming to her aid had she been able to build a respectable life.

As luck would have it, Rex applied for and landed a position in San Diego with Stewart Brothers Architects and Engineers. Having relocated back to his home town, he had his dream job. Best of all, he and Becky could now see each other more often.

Several months later, he and Becky married. The best man, of course, was Jeff. In time Rex got promoted to a senior position at the firm.

Meanwhile, Jeff continued in his job learning, working hard, and playing hard.

One day Jeff received an unexpected phone call. "How would you like to go into business for yourself?" Rex asked.

Flabbergasted, Jeff replied, "Well, yeah, I guess so; but what's the deal?"

"The Stewart Brothers are ready to retire and want to sell their firm. They are giving me first crack at it. Here's their offer: they want one million in cash up front and ten percent of our gross profit each year over the next three years. I know that sounds like too much to overcome, but it's a steal. I have already gone over the books with my accountant. It's sound! Can you come up with a half million?"

"I don't think so, Rex. But, you sound like you know what you're talking about. So, yeah, I'll bust my ass trying. Let me see what I can do, and I'll get back with you."

Rex's future would not be fulfilled until he became an entrepreneur. Before his family relocated to San Diego, they had owned the only dry goods store in Wapiti Valley, a small town in Northern California. Rex had spent a good part of his teen years honing his business skills there. His evolvement into this latest endeavor was all too predictable.

Jeff had been caught off guard and unsure about his options. *Let's see. Withdraw funds from my 401K. Sell my condo. Sell my BMW. Borrow from my bank. I'll still be about two hundred thousand shy.*

The only source left was his family – and that presented a distasteful task he really did not want to pursue. Nevertheless, he decided to swallow his pride and go after it.

Jeff arranged a quick trip to Colorado. His dad met him at the Denver International Airport and drove him the 68 miles to Carson Springs. It had been almost two years since they had seen each other, so it was a joyful meeting.

En route, Mr. Benson began the conversation by explaining that he had lost his business. "Jeff, I told you that I had liquidated all the merchandise in my pharmacy."

"Yeah, and I felt really bad when you told me."

"It's not as bad as you might think. Actually, it's a blessing. I'm working only 20 hours a week now, instead of the 70 to 80 I worked before. Wal-Mart forced me out of business and now I'm filling prescriptions for them. How's that for a weird change?"

"Well, as long as you're happy, that's all that matters. Is Mom okay with the change?"

"She's happier than I am."

Jeff nodded. "I'm eager to gorge myself on her spare ribs and kraut. You know, I could be blindfolded in our neighborhood and still find my way home just by the telltale aromas from her kitchen."

Martha Benson had the reputation of being one of the best cooks in the community. She was a stay-at-home mom and devoted a lot of her time to perfecting her cooking skills. The local churches and clubs were always glad when she brought her dishes to their events.

Once inside the house, Jeff said, "Dad, I told you on the phone about the dilemma I'm facing. I need to somehow come up with about 200 grand."

"Son, I wish you had told me sooner. I had a $300 thousand variable annuity we could have tapped, but that's not an option now. I let a slick talking broker convince me to exchange my annuity without surrender charges for one that has a seven year surrender penalty."

"That's too bad. What's his name?"

"I still have his business card." Mr. Benson walked over to his old and weathered roll top desk. "Here it is: Richard M. Draff, with offices in Denver and Indiana."

Jeff offered, "Maybe we can go to arbitration and get a settlement."

"Well, right now I would say your best bet would be to go in and see Joe Kilbourne."

Joe had been a high school classmate of Jeff's, and was now the president of First Buffalo Bank. Joe had been the class valedictorian and had received offers of scholarships from numerous colleges. He had ended up at the University of Colorado with a business major. Members of the Kilbourne family were considered "pillars of their community." Joe, of course, shared that reputation. It had been a strong draw to convince him to settle down in Carson Springs.

The only blemish on Joe's reputation had happened when, as a teenager, he and the two Thompson brothers herded a cow into the city jail on Halloween when all the police were out patrolling the city. For awhile no one knew who had been behind the prank, but secrets could not be kept very long in this town. Because they were teens, the boys were not charged with a misdemeanor, but Mr. Kilbourne made Joe perform 50 hours of community service - mostly picking up litter.

Jeff phoned the bank right away to make an appointment with Joe. The next morning he arrived promptly at 10 o'clock.

"Hey, Jeff, how's sunny California treating you these days?"

"Fine, but it's always good to get back here for a visit."

"What can I do for you?"

"I'm in desperate need of 200 grand. It's for a business that my partner and I want to buy."

"Jeff, even without asking you all the particulars, I know you are not one to come up with frivolous ideas. Your dad took out the limit on his life insurance policy for David when he was in med school. So that can't be used for collateral. I can give you a second on his home, but one hundred is the most I could go. Even that would mean stretching the home's value, and it includes 25 thousand on your signature."

"Okay, thanks. You're a real pal. I'll take whatever I can get and hope somehow I can find a way for the rest. Say hello to your mom and dad."

Jeff allowed extra days for his visit so he could take in the town as a way of relaxation and maybe feel some nostalgia. Many of the sights remained as he remembered; however some of the boarded up store fronts caused a feeling of sadness. His dad's pharmacy was now serving as a temporary tax preparation office.

It was Saturday, and downtown was devoid of the crowds he remembered. He especially wanted to see the school and football field only six blocks away. When he arrived there, he paused at a spot on the 42nd yard line, looked down, and closed his eyes. Here was the exact spot where it had happened. Leaping for a pass, he had been upended at the top of his reach. His left foot had flown out, he had pounded the turf with his knee extended in an awkward angle, and he had torn his anterior cruciate ligament. He had had to spend almost a year in rehab. No spring track that year. His 4.4 speed in the forty would be gone forever. So disappointing, yet he was grateful for the successful surgery and eventual recovery.

Returning to the home place, Jeff looked around the yard and the neighborhood. *Well, some things have changed, but not too many.* When he entered the garage his old bike, suspended from the ceiling, caught his attention. Curious to see if it was still serviceable, he discovered that the tires had become dry rotted. At first he nixed any thoughts of riding it. *Hey. Why don't I fix up this old relic with new tires and tubes? No other repairs are needed – maybe just a bit of lubrication. A trip to the local hardware store should do the trick. After a re-tiring I'll be ready to ride.*

*****

Jeff chose a route that covered some of the roads he had traveled years ago on that same bike to deliver prescriptions for his dad. He noticed that new apartments had sprung up along the way, many built for seniors. In this part of town some of the pharmacy's customers could not pay for their drugs. His dad had given specific instructions to never refuse service to anyone, or to badger anyone for payment. *Dad lifted the bar of character to a high pinnacle for David and me to achieve. I trust neither of us will give up trying.*

On Sunday after church, Jeff's mother asked him how he was living and spending his time. "I worry about you. I wish you would get married and settle down."

"Find me a good girl and I will."

"Look around. What about somebody like Lisa Coburn?"

"What? Have you seen how that pretty homecoming queen has let herself go? Seriously, you wouldn't want me to marry a girl that huge, would you?

"That's not the way to look at it. I'm sure she would be a better wife than one of those wild girls out there in California."

"Mom, you're stereotyping. All Californians are not wild party goers. Just like all Texans are not cowboys."

Before he began packing for his return trip, Jeff hugged his mother, hoping to reassure her that he would be okay.

*****

Jeff phoned Rex when he returned to say he was short of the required cash. The ensuing days were fraught with anxiety. It began to appear it would be a "no deal."

Rex and Becky discussed the dilemma with Becky's family, who came forward with the necessary cash – with the understanding that it would be a 60-40 partnership. In addition, her family agreed to provide working capital while the guys were getting the business off the ground.

Finally the day came when Jeff cashed in his assets, resigned from his job, and relocated to San Diego.

CHAPTER THREE

The two proud owners were tempted to use their own names on the business, but knew better than to change the Stewart Brothers' name since it was well known and well respected.

In order to make their firm's name even more recognizable in the community, they participated in job fairs, home shows, and similar venues.

A Southern California show in San Diego featuring community improvements was held at the County Exposition Hall. Entrepreneurship meant everything to Rex, and he took the lead in manning a booth to display several models of their projects.

Next to his booth was an artist well known in the area who was displaying some of her work featuring street scenes in San Diego. Barbara Douglas introduced herself to Rex. Although foot traffic was heavy, they found time to exchange business discussions. Rex admired her talent and ability with the brush. Barbara, in turn, admired Rex's efficient and economical designs that had both purpose and eye appeal.

By the second day their conversations had become more personal.

Rex was overwhelmed by the graciousness and demeanor of Barbara. She seemed to have a perpetual smile. (It was a *Duchenne,* named for the pioneering French neurologist who identified the relevant muscles which involve eyes as well as lips. This smile differs from a social or phony smile.) The friendly tone of her voice magnified self-assurance to any in her presence.

Rex hesitated at first, thinking she might consider him too forward. Finally he spoke his thoughts. "I have a partner who would like to make your acquaintance."

'And who would that be?"

"His name is Jeff ... Jeff Benson. I have your business card. Would it be too presumptuous for me to tell him to call you?"

"No, not at all."

Over the weekend, Rex talked to Becky about the lady he had just met. She could feel the excitement in his voice when he described her.

"Do you think Jeff will be interested in an artist?"

"Anyone would be interested in her. She's that special."

As soon as Jeff arrived at the office on Monday morning, Rex began describing his weekend encounter.

"You say she's an artist? What in heaven's name would I have in common with an artist?"

"Maybe not with her work, but I'm telling you, you'll really like her."

"Is she pretty?"

"Pretty enough. Her real beauty is within. Take my word for it, Jeff, she's a keeper. If you really want to know about her physical features, she's about five foot nine, 135-140 pounds. Very natural looking. Long auburn hair almost to her waistline.

Blue/gray eyes and her teeth are white-white. She stands erect, which gives her an athletic look without diminishing her femininity. Oh yeah, she's pretty. Not beautiful, but very pretty."

"Okay, I'm convinced. Give me her number."

Jeff waited several days before he called. He didn't want to appear too eager. When he did call, she answered with a pleasant hello. Her "hello" was not only pleasant; it was also a hidden identification of her character. The tone in that one word was enough for him to form a favorable first impression.

"Is this Barbara?"

"Yes."

"I'm Jeff. I believe my partner Rex mentioned me to you. He told me about you, and I'd like for us to meet. Say, what about you and I having dinner together?"

"I'm sorry. I don't go on blind dates."

Jeff waited a few moments. "Oh...well, is there any way we could get together? Right now I don't have a 'Plan B.'"

"Perhaps a lunch?"

"Sounds good to me."

"How about Friday at noon?"

"It's a deal. Do you have a favorite place?"

"Would Sullivan's be okay?"

"Fine."

Barbara said, "I'll be wearing a beige pantsuit trimmed in yellow."

Jeff responded, "I'll don a Greek fisherman's cap."

Sullivan's was an upscale casual restaurant, a favorite with many of the locals. Jeff arrived shortly after noon, and Barbara soon followed.

Jeff had never been one to believe in love at first sight, but with the countenance surrounding her smiling face and the brightness of her eyes focused directly on him, he felt an uncontrollable emptiness inside. To keep from staring, he had to look away; yet he did not want to avoid her. *I know this feeling cannot be love, but what is it? Something strange is happening ... it's mysterious. It feels like I am in the presence of a spirit.* He was so confused, all he could do was mutter, "Oh, what a pleasant surprise to meet you."

Jeff and Barbara introduced themselves again and were seated promptly.

Jeff was finally able to start a conversation. "Rex told me about your art work. Is that your main vocation?"

"Yes. I started painting when I was very young. Maybe it's part of my DNA. My parents encouraged me to pursue this interest by providing me with a good education in art. Unfortunately, both my mother and my dad were killed in a car accident when I was 15. A drunk driver hit them head-on."

"I'm so sorry," Jeff interrupted.

"I was an only child. Maybe spoiled but I never considered myself bratty. My grandfather took over as a parent and he arranged for me to attend the Pratt Institute of Art in New York City.

"What about your grandfather now?" Jeff interrupted again.

"He's semiretired. Lives in a condo on a golf course in Monterey. He staked me while I was starting out. After struggling through my 'starving artist' period, I won approval for my paintings and my career took off. Later I was invited to the Cranbrook Academy in Michigan for a summer workshop, which was too awesome. My art education set me on a course I couldn't leave. The instruction was from world acclaimed artists.

"Am I bragging now?" She rolled her eyes and nearly dropped her fork, then continued: "And a summer in Paris didn't hurt my art development. Oh, how I loved Paris. I could return tomorrow."

"Exciting times, no doubt? How about your other interests?"

"Jeff, are you wanting me to do all the talking?"

He studied her as he'd been doing from the first sight of her, captivated by her beauty, her warm smile, and the sparkle in her eyes. He did not notice the tentativeness of her actions or the faltering words she spoke. His only perception was of her tantalizing presence.

"I suppose Rex told you about our business and how we met in a co-op program while we were attending the same college. We make a good team. He's like a brother to me.

"What do you do when you're not painting?"

"Well, I golf once a week at Whispering Pines. I'm in a ladies' league, and we play every Wednesday morning.

"Are you a good golfer?"

"Sometimes. I have a four handicap."

She explained further that her dad had attended Wake Forest on a golf scholarship and had taken a job as a pro at Whispering Pines after graduation. He had left her a lifetime membership there.

"Do you play golf, Jeff?"

"Yes, but not much lately. I played some in college. I became interested when I caddied as a kid. I don't have an established handicap. History takes up much of my leisure time. I'm a seasoned history buff."

"Do you have brothers or sisters?"

"I have one brother. He just finished his residency and has a practice in internal medicine in Seattle."

Jeff and Barbara finished lunch and left the restaurant without any mention of a follow-up.

Barbara entered her impressions of the time with Jeff in her diary just as soon as she arrived home, afraid she would have a lapse in memory if she waited until the next day.

*****

Friday 8/4

Dear Diary, My luncheon date with Jeff Benson was most enjoyable. He appeared up tight in the beginning (even more than I was) but soon appeared more relaxed. He came across with an even temperament. His politeness probably reflects his small town upbringing. — Seemed genuinely attuned to my conversation about my art career and my golf. He's aggressive yet not belligerent. I should also mention his athletic physique and the way he carries himself — not a swagger, but still full of confidence. Lastly, he would be a great catch for any gal!

*****

Jeff called again in a few days. This time he offered a dinner/dance date at the Mid-Manhattan.

"I'll come by around seven, okay?"

"Yeah, let me give you directions to my place."

Barbara's home/studio was situated in a tranquil setting which allowed for a minimum of noise and interruptions. The first floor was mainly a living area with a small offset used for business. The atelier upstairs extended the full length of the house. It was filled with an abundance of paintings and art supplies. Viewed from the outside, at a distance, the triangular windows dominated the architectural features, covering both the east and west sides. Viewed from the inside, there was a vista leading to a wooded hill. The grounds had an informal appearance, yet were well maintained. Bougainvilleas, hibiscus and orchids were the prominent landscape features.

Barbara decided not to offer a tour of the premises, holding that for a later visit.

The Mid-Manhattan had separate booths which provided the right setting for small talk. It had a tiny dance floor. Both Barbara and Jeff displayed their top dancing talents – his the tango, hers the waltz. They agreed upon Blue Pointe oysters on the half shell as their appetizer. For her entree, Barbara opted for the broiled halibut, and Jeff chose steak and potatoes. At that point food became the topic of conversation. He explained that he had always been a meat and potatoes guy – no quiche for him.

Jeff felt now was the time to say it: "I do not eat chicken in any form. Telling you now might save any embarrassment later on."

Barbara laughed. "I'm glad you told me. I wouldn't want to force any particular food on anyone."

"For me, this is no laughing matter," Jeff said earnestly. He began to tell her about the time that led to his embarrassment over food. Friends, Bob and Elaine, had invited him and his then girlfriend to dinner. Elaine, eager to show off her epicurean talents, had gone to great lengths in preparing this meal. Jeff had been at ease until the platter of Cornish hens with vichyssoise was passed. He first had thought he might feign some sort of dietary excuse, then had had second thoughts. After trying to conceal picks, stirs and tumbles with his fork, he could no longer pretend when Bob had asked him the obvious. Bob had scolded Elaine right then and there for her choice of the main dish. Jeff had wanted to slink under the table and disappear. He had made a pact with himself then that he would never be in that predicament again. Better to state his dislike for chicken, the sooner the better, regardless of etiquette advices.

Jeff looked directly into Barbara's face to tell her, "I've enjoyed your company. Everything was great, not to mention the delicious dinner." The evening ended with no mention of a follow up.

*****

Fri 8/11

Dear Diary — another enjoyable time with Jeff. He displayed an emphatic point about his dislike for chicken — almost to a loud outcry. We seemed to be in rhythm with the dances. He's really great with the tango.

*****

Rex wanted Jeff to be pleased with the matchmaking he had initiated. "What do you think about Barbara?"

"She's okay. I like her."

"I knew you would. Will you continue dating her?"

"Depends. We're different. I'll just have to see how things work out."

"Has she asked about your work or business?"

"She alluded to it, but somehow I didn't follow up on it."

"You dummy!" Rex shouted. "That would have been an ideal way to bridge the differences between you two."

"Kick me! I'll pursue that real soon."

*****

Next, Jeff and Barbara got together for a visit to the world famous San Diego Zoo. The day gave them a respite from having so much conversation centered on themselves. After several winding walks between cages and enclosures, they became weary and sat on a shady bench. They enjoyed the noisy laughter and chatter of a group of kids from a nearby children's home – until the loud roar of a lion completely silenced them all.

*****

As they were leaving the zoo, Jeff remembered the advice given to him by Rex, and suggested that they go to his office. Without hesitation, Barbara responded, "Yeah, let's go. I am curious about your work."

The one story brick building had an office at the entry and a "shop" extending beyond for one hundred feet or so. The grounds were landscaped to perfection with just the right balance of color and form.

Jeff was eager to show her around, and for her to see the work area where he spent most of his time. Then, on to a shop filled with drafting desks, computers, and structural models.

Jeff was proud of how far the business had come in the few years since he and Rex had taken over.

"What do you know about engineering and architecture?" he asked.

"Very little. Several of the art courses I took emphasized architecture in cityscape paintings. But tell me about your projects."

"Here are some pictures. As you can see, they cover shopping centers, hospitals, and schools. If you go past the west side of Mission Street, you'll see the Asiatic Trade Center. That's one of our recent jobs."

He continued, "When we are awarded a project we are not always the low bidder. We stand behind our work, and our honesty and integrity are well known. When something goes wrong, as it often does – you know Murphy's Law – there's always a lot of the blame game taking place. Whose fault is it? Is it us, or is it the contractor, the sub-contractor, the vendor, or the supplies or equipment? When we make a mistake, we admit it up front and go ahead with our corrections. That practice doesn't go unnoticed. It helps us win bids."

"What other structures have you built?"

"The next time you go up to Ocean City, check out their municipal building."

"I will. I'm up there often."

She left with a better appreciation of his work.

*****

Sat 8/20

Dear Diary, without analyzing Jeff's psyche, I've concluded that he is so much more well rounded for an engineer than I would have expected. Obviously, his brain hemispheres are more equal because he has a bent toward the verbal, the arts, and such. He's beginning to grow on me. I could not shake him off now, even if I wanted to. I want to show my affection without being pushy. I really like that guy! He's cool!"

*****

Jeff was surprised to receive a phone call from Barbara the next day inviting him to join her for a round of golf. "Would you care to play with me next Saturday morning?"

He was elated, knowing that their friendship was gaining ground and that she was not so coy in moving things forward. "Yes," he answered, trying not to show his exuberance, "I'll take you up on that."

"Okay, then, it's all set. We'll meet at the pro shop, say nine o'clock?"

"I'll be there."

On Saturday morning, they met as planned. Barbara was obviously a familiar fixture at the clubhouse. She gave Jeff a short tour and orientation of the place, then introduced him to Jack Owens, the club pro.

"Take good care of him, Jack. You will no doubt be seeing more of him."

"Yeah, it might be for lessons," Jeff grinned.

Barbara later directed Jeff to a locker room attendant. He changed shoes, and then met Barbara at the number one tee. He was a bit perplexed when he saw Barbara step up to the men's tee.

"Do you always use the men's tee?"

"Yes, except when I'm playing in a ladies' tournament. I want the game to be a challenge."

"It's already too much of a challenge for me," Jeff offered.

The first hole was a par four, straight, but with strategically placed bunkers on both sides. Barbara drove 240 yards, laser straight, down the middle of the fairway. Jeff's effort was not too bad, 210 yards, almost into the left bunker. She parred the hole and he bogied.

When the round was completed, she had scored a 74, two over par. He had managed an 85, thirteen over.

"You did okay, especially considering you've been away from the game, Jeff."

"Your game is something to behold, Barbara. You should go on tour."

She laughed. "No, that's not for me."

"I have a video of Sam Snead. You know, your swing is much like his."

"Thanks. That's a good compliment."

CHAPTER FOUR

Jeff and Barbara continued to date, and soon became almost inseparable.

Jeff planned a beach party, to include Rex and Becky. He called Barbara, only to hear her give a polite refusal. "I'll be attending an art auction for the next few days. I'm leaving tomorrow and won't return until Monday next week."

"Where are you going?"

"Taos, New Mexico."

"Oh, that artsy place. How are you traveling?"

"I'll take my van. Need to protect my paintings."

"I'll miss you, Barbara."

"I'll miss you, too."

*****

Barbara arrived at Taos the next day after an exhausting trip interrupted by a dust storm. Once she was sure that her art had survived without damage, she settled into the warm greetings of Chloe Clement. Barbara did not expect to see Chloe adorned in anything but buckskin, and she was not disappointed. A Stetson on top and boots below helped Chloe reach five feet four.

The two women had developed a close friendship. It had started from a mix-up in motel reservations four years earlier. When Barbara found herself without a place to stay, she saw Chloe's notice on a bulletin board in the Taos town square, listing a spare bedroom for rent. Barbara was glad to take it rather than travel 20 miles away to look for other lodging.

The invitation to stay at her home had been repeated by Chloe every year since.

How could two people so dissimilar find ways to become close friends? It appears Chloe was in awe of Barbara's art and the huge bids she received at the auctions, especially contrasted with the much smaller bids for her own watercolors. Barbara, on the other hand, reveled in Chloe's antics. Her friend was a-laugh-a-minute.

Chloe, a confirmed spinster in her fifties, had relocated to Taos from a small town called Chew-and-Tell, Texas. Her bio would read like a cowgirl who never stopped long enough to allow any of her three brothers to outdo her in bareback riding or steer roping. Coarse, off color language suited her demeanor, no doubt coming from her association with the rodeo crowd. All of this led to a successful rodeo promotion career.

A permanent disability resulting from her being thrown from a bucking horse had left her unable to perform the physical demands of riding and roping or even managing rodeo shows. During her convalescence she had become hooked on watercolor painting and never went back to the rodeo circuit.

*****

The first day turnout for the auction at the Assembly Hall was heavy. Barbara received these bids for her art:

"Spring Awakening" –succulents blooming after a heavy rain - $1,200.

"Adobe Sweet Home" –a small home isolated at the foot of a towering mountain - $3,500.

"Saguaro Sentries" – dozens of cacti in upright attendance, $21,000.

And "Santa Fe at Sunset" – subdued colors accentuated against the red-orange horizon - $2,200.

As Barbara stepped outside the Assembly Hall she noticed a crowd gathered around Chloe, who was entertaining them with her palomino, "Charlie." The horse was showing off his stunts, prancing, kneeling, and finally kissing Chloe. Chloe was telling jokes while she danced through her lasso *ala* Will Rogers.

"I kept having a problem and needed help with my hearing. I told the doc, 'My hearing is so bad I can't hear myself fart.' The doc appeared to be very helpful. He sidled over to the medicine cabinet, reached in and grabbed a handful of pills. When I looked at them, I was astounded. Those pills were the size of gum-balls! I asked, 'Doc, will these pills really make me hear better?' The doc replied: 'No, they will just make you fart louder!'"

The crowd's jubilant response kept Chloe hopping through her lasso and telling more jokes.

*****

The following day, Barbara drove 210 miles to the Toqja Indian Reservation, impatient to report good news to the tribe.

Chief Grey Lobo greeted her warmly, always glad to see her. "Welcome again, Barbara. It's a real pleasure to see you. Will you be able to stay awhile?"

"Not this time, Chief. I need to get back home. But here's my news: I've added $8,000 to the scholarship endowment."

"Good!" he exclaimed. "How wonderful. You must stay long enough to meet your latest scholarship recipient."

The chief hailed a small boy and asked him to retrieve the girl, a pretty, rather shy 17 year old.

"Barbara, meet Betty Blue Sky."

"I'm so glad to meet you, Betty. What do you plan to study? Have you decided on a college?

"I haven't decided on a school yet, but I think I would like to be a veterinarian."

"That's wonderful. There should be much demand for that profession. Good luck!"

CHAPTER FIVE

When Barbara returned home, Jeff was interested to learn how the trip had worked out. "Did you sell all your paintings?"

"Yes, I have come back empty handed."

"Do you go to this auction every year?"

"Not really. I go when I feel it's a good time. Many of my paintings depict southwestern scenes, and Taos is a good location for those kinds of sales. Also, it's convenient to the Toqja Indian Reservation."

"Indian reservation?!"

"Yes. I haven't mentioned this to you before, but the American Indian is very close to my heart. Some of my ancestors were Indian."

"Really?"

Barbara's great-great-grandmother, Nocutana, four generations removed, was a Cherokee Indian who lived in

Southeastern Tennessee. She had been part of the forced removal of Cherokees from their lands, when the Federal government had ordered 30,000 of them to relocate to Oklahoma. Her tribe had been rounded up along with others from Western North Carolina and Northern Georgia. They had been placed in stockades at Calhoun, Tennessee before being forced to walk the thousand miles or more to the reservation. Many perished on the long trip, which became known as the infamous "Trail of Tears."

After Barbara recounted this story to Jeff, he inquired, "Weren't the Cherokees protected by treaties?"

"Yes, and they took the State of Georgia to court, but they lost. The US Supreme Court overruled the lower court in favor of the Indians. But then President Andrew Jackson said – reputedly – 'John Marshall made his decision – now let him enforce it.'"

This is a depiction of how the U. S. Government dealt with native Americans who would not heed their tyranny:

Chiefs, head men, warriors! Will you then by resistance compel us to resort to arms? God forbid! Or will you by flight, seek to hide ourselves in mountains and forests, and thus oblige us to hunt you down? Remember that, in pursuit, it may be impossible to avoid conflicts. The blood of the white man or the blood of the red man may be spilt, and if spilt, however accidentally, it may be impossible for the discrete and human among you, or among us, to prevent a general war and carnage. Think of this my Cherokee brethren! I am an old warrior, and I have been present at many a scene of slaughter: but spare me, I beseech you, the horror of witnessing the destruction of the Cherokee." [1]

---

[1] General Winfield Scott, May 10, 1838. (New American State papers. 1789-1860 – 1972, 10:126.)

Barbara continued, "I owe my existence to Nocutana's will and determination to survive."

"How did you find out about your ancestry and all of this?"

"Through intensive searches in courthouse documents, Federal government archives, and the Mormon Church's genealogical records."

"What happened to the Cherokee after they reached Oklahoma?"

"I know only about my great-great-grandmother. She married another Cherokee, and all their offspring married persons of European descent.

"Now you know why I feel a close kinship to Native Americans and why I have taken such an interest in them."

"I do understand."

Jeff was intrigued by her story and found Barbara much different than any of his former girlfriends. It was at this moment he knew she was someone he wanted to know much better.

CHAPTER SIX

Rex and Becky thought it would be a good idea for the four of them to get in a round of golf. Rex posed the idea to Barbara and suggested the next Saturday morning.

"I wish I could. Let me give you a rain check. Saturday morning I'll be teaching an art class for a bunch of kids from the inner city."

Rex asked, "How do you find time for all these things?"

"I try to be organized; plus, I have a few advantages."

"Such as?"

"For starters, I work out of my home which means I save time by not commuting. And, would you believe I've never been to a beauty shop? Also, my grandfather handles all my finances, including the scholarship fund for the Toqjas."

"Tell us more about your grandfather."

"He handles asset management accounts for a dozen or so clients. His track record generates a long waiting list. I like the fact that, in addition to his designations as CPA and CFP, he's a Registered Investment Advisor. That means he works on a fee basis, rather than on commission. He has a fiduciary relationship with his clients."

*****

As Jeff and Barbara's courtship continued over the next several months, their love for one another grew more and more intense. Jeff was not sure how he had come to love Barbara, but he knew now that he wanted to spend the rest of his life with her.

"Barbara, we are so different in our work and certain likes and dislikes; I can't explain why we are so much in love. I don't know any other way to say this, but I want to marry you."

"We may be more alike than you realize, Jeff. We share the same values that each of us honors and respects."

"I'd never thought of it that way, but you're right."

CHAPTER SEVEN

Several months later, Barbara received a surprise phone call. "Hello, is this Barbara Douglas?"

"Yes."

"I'm Frank Oppenheimer, the CEO of Maywood Hospitalities, calling from Chicago. I have a gift for you."

"A gift? What kind of gift?"

"I've just returned from an inspection trip to the Hotel King Carlos.in San Diego. The manager there showed me your wedding announcement in the local paper. Have you made your final arrangements yet?"

"No, but we're getting close."

"Our company is offering you and your groom a two night stay in our Presidential Suite complete with all the amenities."

"I don't know what to say. How did I come into this good fortune?"

"I was made aware of your civic work, especially with your art auctions to benefit the United Way. By the way, I am in our board room at this moment looking at your painting of downtown San Diego. The King Carlos is predominant."

"Thank you so much. We will definitely take you up on this generous offer. I'll run it by Jeff, but I know he'll be just as pleased as I am."

*****

The wedding party of 250 included Rex and Becky, family members, friends from the golf league, church, neighbors, business clients, city officials, and of course Chief Grey Lobo and his family. The small Rock of Ages Church overflowed.

A reception was held later that day at the Whispering Pines. Jeff's family covered the cost of the food and music; Barbara's grandfather paid for their trip to Hawaii.

It was nearly nine o'clock when the couple finally left. A limo took them to the King Carlos Hotel – by far the premier hotel in the city. Built in the 1930's at the height of the depression, it had never struggled financially as many others did. Its clientele included the wealthy and super wealthy who had anticipated a downturn in the economy and had acted prudently. It had been updated regularly to keep it attuned to the times. The stunning decor, including sculptures and paintings by outstanding artists of the time, gave it an opulence to admire.

As they walked in to the stately hotel entrance, Jeff and Barbara were awed by gilded Corinthian columns and art deco floor mosaics.

"Oh, how beautiful," Barbara remarked as they toured the spacious lobby.

The gracious hotel staff awaited them, and an attendant introduced himself as their personal valet. He handed them a list of amenities and said, "Just dial 27 and I will be at your service."

Their luggage was already there when Jeff and Barbara entered their huge suite. Murals adorned the high walls, depicting some of the city's history of Spanish missions. A separate dining room boasted a wine rack and cooler complete with vintage imports from around the world. Delicious-looking hors d'oeuvres were displayed on fine china.

"Look!" Jeff pointed to a set of wine glasses decorated with the hotel's logo and etched with their initials. An attached note read, "Keep these with our compliments."

A large log burning in the fireplace completed the romantic setting.

After they toasted their happiness and enduring love, Barbara excused herself. She returned to the room adorned only in an ivory shade mesh negligee trimmed in gold colored lace. By that time Jeff had half undressed.

She whispered, "Do you like what you see?"

Jeff was so enthralled he could not choose words to speak, but silently took her hand and led her across to the bedroom. He finished undressing, flicked the light off at the switch, and pulled her closer. They embraced, kissing repeatedly. Attempting to see her facial expression, Jeff gently pushed Barbara away to see her at arms' length. The room was almost dark except for the moonlight beaming through the window. The backlighting shining on Barbara created an aura of enchantment and beauty like he had never seen before. It shone on her waist length hair, causing it to glisten as if in twilight. He brought her back into a close embrace once again, their kisses becoming more passionate.

"Yes." He finally answered. "I like what I see."

Jeff wanted this night to last forever.

CHAPTER EIGHT

One week of honeymooning in Hawaii flew by, but not before Jeff and Barbara covered most of the attractions. Soon after their arrival they rented a car and encircled the entire island of Oahu on a trip that took less than six hours. Later in the week they filled a morning with surfing on the northern end of the island. Their visit was capped by a memorable afternoon at Pearl Harbor to witness a ceremony eulogizing those American sailors still entombed in the sunken USS Arizona battleship.

Kodak sponsored a photo event with a chorus line of hula dancers. Jeff joined them for picture taking, only after Barbara's persistent coaxing.

*****

Back from Hawaii, the two began to settle in to their work. The time spent away had been leisure at its best. Maybe too much time to think and reflect. Jeff sensed that the image of Barbara on their wedding night was some kind of *deja vu*. He wondered, *What was causing all this? A spirit? Or had there been a time in his past when this same thing happened? Could it be an event incarnated from another world?* Jeff faced an enigma he could not fathom. *Perhaps in time the answer will emerge.*

Jeff moved into Barbara's house, which provided him an easy commute. They often got together with Rex and Becky for golf. The two women became close friends, blending easily with the men. The congeniality among them was obvious to their other friends. One couple dubbed them the "rat pack."

An unanticipated notice arrived in the mail, informing Jeff that his loan from the First Buffalo Bank in Carson Springs had been paid off, releasing both him and his dad from the debt. He let out a big yell, eager to spread the news. Having the debt paid off gave him great satisfaction.

The papers enclosed with the letter carried a Nashville, Tennessee address. At first Jeff deemed the papers to be of no consequence, but as he began to file them away, a thought came to him in an odd way; you could even say a spiritual way. *Yes! What a revelation! Bingo! That's it! Now I know! It was that high school history class field trip to Nashville to visit the Parthenon.*

Jeff quickly dug out the post cards and other literature he had stashed away from that trip. He sat down at his desk as he read:

The Parthenon was the chief temple in the Acropolis in Athens, Greece. Work began in 447 B.C. and was completed in 432 B.C., at which time the statue of Athena was dedicated. Measuring 101.34 by 228.14 feet, it represented the peak of the Greek Doric Order. Before being placed in the Parthenon, Athena was widely worshipped in homes and palaces. The choice of the location of her dwelling in the Acropolis stemmed from the location there of the king's palace.

In Homer's *Iliad*, Athena inspired and fought alongside warriors. With Achaean, she strengthened him when he was wounded and even guided his spear, a symbol of prowess.

When divinity appeared and inspired a man to guide his hand to great accomplishments this deity should be a female.

Though Athena and Zeus strive for prominence, she stands above and alone.

Jeff knew that the Nashville Parthenon is an exact replica of the ancient Greek structure. Athena, a sculpture adorned in gold and ivory stands forty-two feet tall at one end. Visiting this wonder had been an exhilarating experience and he had never forgotten it. Barbara's similar adornments of gold and ivory tones had exhibited the same look and aura on their wedding night. Both women were majestic, and both had etched an indelible memory in his mind.

The Greeks had their goddess and I have mine.

CHAPTER NINE

Barbara, being curious about the progress of Betty Blue Sky, placed a phone call to Chief Grey Lobo.

"How's my Betty doing in her school work?"

"Betty is doing just fine. I'm glad you called, because I want to tell you about an upcoming special event. All Souls' Day will be celebrated by our tribe on November 2nd. We want to honor you on that day for the many contributions you've made to our people."

"How nice. What kind of honor?"

"We want to make you an honorary Cherokee. Can you come?"

"Let's see, that's two weeks from now on a Thursday. Yes, I can make it, but please don't go to any trouble."

"It will be our pleasure."

Barbara insisted that Jeff accompany her to witness the moment, and he enthusiastically obliged.

Chief Grey Lobo wanted this occasion to be authentic. Accordingly, he contacted a friend, John Campbell, a full-blooded Cherokee from Oklahoma who was a Council member with authority to perform certain honorary acts according to Cherokee customs.

Jeff and Barbara arrived late in the day, just in time for the feast. Chief Grey Lobo directed them to a gathering place called Anadasgisi, which means "they are gathering" in the Cherokee language. In the center was a pyre about six feet in diameter. The entire tribe, including the women and children, took positions in a wide circle around the pyre. Foods included roasted venison, trout, spicy fry-bread, wild greens, and potatoes.

Barbara took a position next to Chief Grey Lobo, and Jeff joined her there. It was completely dark now, with only the licking flames allowing limited vision. A fruit wine was passed from one to another around the circle.

Soon, however, the bright Full Harvest moon -- usually seen in October, not November – rose and shone brightly, with orange dominating its customary yellow glow. In the distance its reflection on the red hilltops was barely visible, but still marked an outline against the dark sky. A single cloud moved under the brightness, diffusing the strong color. This dramatic scene from the nocturnal heavens, eerie as it was beautiful, provided the perfect setting for the ritual which was to follow.

Fulfilling the feeling and mood of this occasion, smoke wafted from the mesquite embers, filling the air with a pleasant embriosity to create a sensual spirituality. Barbara's anticipation grew into nervousness. When Jeff noticed her pale face and blank stare, he reached over; first putting his arms around her waist, then clutching her cold moist hands.

Before the presentation, a dozen young men adorned in their native headdresses began dancing and chanting. The sound of beating drums echoed throughout the area. Their voices could be heard rising above the drums and the ringing bells on their ankles.

When the dancing subsided, Chief Grey Lobo introduced John Campbell, who asked for the Indian Bonnet. The bonnet, decorated in turquoise jewelry with a long eagle feather, was passed among seven tribe members. Each one took the headdress, reverently extended it skyward, then passed it on. When it was finally passed to John Campbell, he asked Barbara to step forward for the presentation.

John Campbell intoned the words, "tsa la gi," meaning, "You are Cherokee." Then he placed the bonnet on Barbara's head.

The young men resumed their dancing and chanting to end the ceremony.

When they returned home, Barbara placed the bonnet in a prominent place next to her plaques and framed certificates of awards and achievements. She knew she would treasure this bonnet more than any of the other awards.

Jeff wanted to know, "Does this mean that you are now a *bona fide* Cherokee?"

"No, it's just honorary."

Happiness followed Barbara and Jeff. Their friendship with Rex and Becky matured, the business partnership thrived, and even their golf scores improved.

Life was oh, so good!

CHAPTER TEN

How was your golf game today, Barbara?" Jeff inquired, as they were in the midst of preparing a spaghetti dinner.

"Not so good. My game seems to be taking a tailspin."

"You might need more lessons from Jack."

"I just don't seem to have the right tempo or rhythm. And lately I've had a sharp pain in my chest and left shoulder."

"What do you think could cause that?"

"I don't know, but if it continues, I'll have it looked at."

Barbara's pain did not go away. Then she noticed a small lump on her shoulder next to her neck. *It's time I find out what's causing the pain. I'm making a doctor's appointment.*

An examination by her family doctor confirmed that the lump needed a further look, and he ordered a biopsy. He referred her to Dr. Shapiro, an oncologist. That same day Barbara travelled to the Oncology Lab at Mercy Hospital. Dr. Shapiro stated, "It doesn't look good to me. Come back Wednesday after the lab makes a determination. You should come with your husband."

The lab expedited their investigation, and concluded that the sample contained cells with non-Hodgkin lymphoma.

Dr. Shapiro and his associate, Dr. Morgan, told Barbara and Jeff the bad news. They were both overcome with sadness, shock, and disbelief.

Jeff blurted, "Are you sure? Can you do another test?"

Dr. Shapiro answered calmly, "We can. But we would get the same results."

"How could this happen?" Jeff asked. "Something strange is going on. There is not a more healthy human being in the whole state of California."

"I can't explain it. These things happen sometimes with no apparent reason."

Barbara took a deep breath, then asked calmly, "What are my odds of survival?"

"You have an aggressive kind of cancer. It's vicious. It spreads quickly."

"But what are my odds?"

"Perhaps 50-50. Maybe not that good."

"Oh, my. I'm not prepared for this."

"We need to start treatments right away. Check into the hospital tomorrow morning. The staff has been notified and they will be ready for you."

Barbara reached for Jeff's hand and grasped it tightly. "Jeff, we've got to be tough. I'm going to beat this thing. I'm sure of that."

*****

Knowing that the cancer was so aggressive, Dr. Shapiro elected to blast it with a powerful initial punch. The treatments caused Barbara to become weak and often nauseated. She began to lose weight, and of course the dying cells in her scalp caused her hair to fall out.

After six weeks, it appeared that the treatments were working. Tests showed no sign of the odd looking cells' reappearing. She was released from the hospital, with Jeff at her side.

Three months passed, and it was still a guessing game about survival. Bad news followed. The cancer had spread to her blood.

After five months, Barbara entered a hospice facility. A chaplain led Jeff to a meditation room, trying to console him, but it was useless. Jeff screamed, "God! My God! How can you do this to me! My greatest love!" Then he began to sob.

One month later Barbara's once strong presence was no more.

Per her explicit request, her remains were cremated. Jeff arranged for a single engine Cessna to scatter her remains over the Toqja reservation.

CHAPTER ELEVEN

Jeff tried hard to contain his grief. He attacked his work energetically to diffuse his constant awareness of his sadness and misery. Rex often caught him late at night and tried unsuccessfully to direct his attention away from the work environment. Jeff's melancholy grew to the point that he developed a serious problem relating to the staff and clients. Rex became very concerned. "Why don't you take a vacation? Go see your brother in Seattle."

"I can't. I just can't seem to get my mind away from Barbara."

His bereavement was not subsiding. Jeff at times would stare into space. His behavior was getting out of control and his work performance was suffering. He struggled on and on, hoping things would change.

Finally, Rex could no longer tolerate what he was seeing, and said, "Jeff, I've made an appointment for you to see a psychiatrist, Dr. Zachery. You need professional help. This can not go on."

"You're right, Rex. Yesterday I had trouble swallowing. I have pain in my knee from that old football injury. Last week I thought I was having a seizure. I do need help. When do I see this doctor?"

"Tuesday at two o'clock."

*****

Jeff arrived at the doctor's office at the appointed time. He was asked by an aide to answer numerous questions about both his physical and mental health. Then Dr. Zachery appeared, introduced himself with an amiable handshake, and invited Jeff to come into his private study. Inside the room an abundance of framed certificates lined the walls. The doctor himself presented an image of competence and confidence. He first allowed Jeff to ramble at length, then began asking personal questions, beginning with, "Tell me about your wife."

"She was too much a part of me. When she died, I felt as though I died, too."

"Do you lapse into memories of her at random times?"

"Yes."

"Do you hallucinate?"

"Yes."

"Do you ever consider yourself to be happy?"

"Almost never."

"Have you dated anyone since your wife died?"

"No."

"Would you like to meet someone to date?"

"Maybe. I'm not sure."

"I have the report from your family physician. There is evidence that your central nervous system is not functioning properly. Please don't be overly alarmed about it now, because we should be able to clear that up."

Several follow-up visits ensued. With each one, the doctor delved more deeply into Jeff's behavior and moods. When he finally gathered enough information, he offered an explanation. "Mr. Benson, your body is in a psychosomatic state. You've developed a physical illness with symptoms lacking a physical cause. We know in your case the symptoms originated in, or were worsened by, your emotional feelings. The medical term is *conversion disorder*. Your diagnosis also includes some characteristics of a somatization disorder which affects the central nervous system. From what you have told me, I suspect that your mind wants to drift you into happier times, but is unable to do so. Your physical body is suffering. I'm prescribing some medication which should help you with your depression. During your next visit we'll try some hypnosis, to see if that might help. At any rate, I feel your long term prognosis is good. With these treatments I believe the psychosomatic illness will disappear."

CHAPTER TWELVE

It was a typical leisurely Saturday morning for Rex and Becky. They enjoyed a country breakfast complete with eggs, sausage, biscuits, juice, jelly and coffee. It was a good break from their hectic and busy work week. Rex read the newspaper sport section in detail and checked the financial section to compute gains and losses on the mutual funds in his IRA.

When the telephone rang to interrupt their morning, Becky offered to take the call in the master bedroom. Upon returning she said, "You'll never guess who that call was from."

"I give up."

"I know you remember my cousin Jayne."

"Oh, yeah, how could I forget?"

"Seems that she is ditching number two and wants to stay here for a couple of days. She's driving from Palm Springs and wants to leave her car here while she goes to Hawaii. You should be glad her husband won't be coming. That was some faux pas you committed at her wedding reception when you mistook him for the sommelier."

"You've got to admit they both looked alike. And I think he would have retrieved the champagne if you hadn't stepped in. Jayne is a real dingbat. I say that even though she is related to you."

"It's a distant relationship."

"Did I tell you how she flirted with me three hours after the ceremony?"

"Many times."

After several moments of silence, Rex faced Becky with a kind of little boy mischievous look. She reciprocated with a Cheshire cat grin.

"Are you thinking the same thing I am?" Rex asked.

"You devil."

"And you're a Jezebel!"

"If we don't succeed, there will be no redemption. If we do, then all will be forgiven."

*****

Jayne arrived the following Friday. Both Rex and Becky welcomed her and made sure she was well accommodated. Becky reserved a table for four at the Old Man and the Sea, an aptly named seafood restaurant. The chit chat proved to be lively and everyone enjoyed the food and fellowship.

When the four of them returned to the Newtons' home at about ten, Becky led the way to the bar area. After a few minutes, Rex excused himself and never returned. Becky soon followed him. Jayne, nursing a scotch and soda, asked Jeff, "Tell me about your business. You and Rex have obviously been very successful."

"Yes, we've done very well."

"Do you spend much time at it, or do you find time for pleasure?"

"I enjoy meeting with my clients and reading history."

"You know what they say about all work and no play. But I don't think you're a dull boy. You seem more like the strong silent type."

"Really?"

"Have you enjoyed being with me?"

"Yes."

"Do you find me attractive?"

"Yes."

"What are you staring at?"

"I'm sorry, I was thinking about something aside from our conversation."

"Would you like to get to know me better?"

"It's getting late. I need to leave."

"Why? Tomorrow is not a work day. What if I moved closer to you? Would you like me even more?"

"I'm leaving."

"Do you shun all your girlfriends this way?"

"I don't have any girlfriends."

"I'm beginning to get the picture."

"Good bye. Nice to have met you."

The next morning Jayne was awaiting the taxi to take her to the airport. Becky was curious about the time she and Jeff had spent together.

"How did it go with Jeff, Jayne?"

"You know, I think Rex's business partner is a swell guy. But you should know he's gay."

"Gay? No, you're wrong about that. He's just going through some tough times. Your taxi's here. Have a good trip."

PART TWO

CHAPTER THIRTEEN

The Droftan University Campus Valentine Party was into its second hour. Frivolity was accented by the amount and variety of spirits being consumed. Marcia Leed and Philip Lockhart were deep into the party, dancing, toasting, and laughing. As the third hour approached, Philip began showing the effects of his drinking; first slurring his speech, then tripping on the dance floor. Marcia allowed him no more alcohol, ignoring his strongly worded objections. An argument ensued, and she whisked him over to a quiet corner.

Marcia considered it a stroke of luck when Fred Bergren appeared. He offered to drive them back to their dorms and she gladly accepted. First he dropped off Philip, then after a short distance he dropped off Marcia. She thanked Fred and was grateful that she had not been driven home by a drunk driver.

When Phil phoned the next day to apologize and to ask for a return date, Marcia accepted his apology but refused to consider any future meetings. She left no doubt their friendship had ended.

*****

Students hurrying from place to place were a clear sign the spring semester was underway at Droftan University. The campus book store was the busiest place, with long lines in front of its vast array of books and electronic gadgets.

As Fred fell in line at the checkout counter, he noticed a familiar face in the adjoining line. How could he not recognize that tall, vivacious, auburn haired beauty? And when Marcia smiled, Fred felt his heart skip, and he couldn't stop staring. They exchanged "hi's" and completed their purchases.

When they reached the outer corridor, Marcia raced to catch up with Fred. "I want to thank you for coming to my aid."

"I was glad to help. Your friend was in no condition to drive you home. By the way, I'm Fred Bergren in case I didn't mention my name before."

"I'm Marcia Leed. Glad to make your acquaintance. I see from you purchases that we must be taking the same computer course. I'm in third period at Thaxton Hall. How 'bout you?"

"Let's see. I don't remember. Oh yes, here it is – third period. Maybe we can compare notes."

"That would be great."

"Bye for now."

It naturally happened that Fred and Marcia met throughout campus locations aside from the one computer class. Fred was not oblivious to a new friendship being formed, and he seized on every opportunity to improve on it. Their friendly encounters evolved into movies, parties, study time, and just strolls together.

Fred was smitten, to say the least, and he pursued any and all ways to enhance their romance. He gifted her on every occasion with jewelry and dined her at expensive restaurants. He said he felt obligated because of her ever present assistance to him on complex class assignments, and he wanted to show his appreciation in identifiable ways. Marcia liked Fred and enjoyed his company; however, his closeness confined her freedom and often made her feel uncomfortable. It was obvious that Fred wanted a serious relationship, but Marcia, who was just turning twenty, was not ready to commit. After several months of courtship, Fred felt confident enough to present her with an engagement ring. Marcia accepted it, although not wholeheartedly.

Fred was eager to show her off to his parents. During spring break, they traveled to Fred's home in Montana.

Looking down from the sky above the Great Falls International Airport, they could see white in the mountains, white in the lowlands – white everywhere. A mid-April blizzard had passed through only two days before, and it had left its mark.

One of Fred's cousins greeted them at the gate and took care of their luggage. They stepped into the Jeep, circled around Great Falls, and entered Highway 87. The roads were clear and the sun was shining, adding a warm feeling to the frigid eighteen-degree weather.

About one hundred miles northeast of the airport, they drove through Lewistown – population less than 12,000. Fred explained to Marcia that the town had been named after Merriweather Lewis, of the famous Lewis and Clark expedition. Past Lewistown, the landscape became barren, with few trees or structures showing above the flat landscape.

"Where are all the people? The houses? The towns?" Marcia asked.

Fred chuckled. "Looks like we left them in Lewistown."

Marcia was like a small kid, wanting to know "When will we get there?" After miles and miles of snow covered plains, they finally arrived at the Bergren's home.

Can you imagine the surprise – a real jaw dropper – when Marcia got her first glimpse of the ranch? Expecting to see an elongated one-story wooden frame house, she was frozen in awe. A fifty foot wide allee, three hundred yards long and lined with

Douglas firs, led to the front entrance of a huge Georgian Colonial that could have been named "Tara."

Once inside, Marcia was given a big bear hug by Fred's father, Victor.

"Meet Marcia, Dad."

"I knew Fred had a keen eye for pretty girls."

Fred's mother appeared and introduced herself. "I'm Margaret."

Margaret showed Marcia to her bedroom, making sure to let her know that it was separate from Fred's room. She was much less enthusiastic about meeting Fred's girlfriend than Victor had been.

Victor excused himself. "I'm in the middle of a cattle transaction," he explained. I have to go back and finish it." He returned to his "War Room," an area filled with phones, weather monitors, computers, printers, and charts.

The wealth of the Bergrens was readily apparent to Marcia; however, their manner was unassuming.

During dinner, the conversation initially centered on Fred. Victor wanted to know, "Are you learning anything from your Ag Engineering courses at school?"

"Sure am. There's much practicality in them."

"Anything that would benefit us?

"I think so. I worked on one project to convert farm machinery from gasoline to natural gas. Another one was to produce electricity by building a small dam. We could do that down on Clear Creek."

"Amazing! Amazing! If we could do those things, we could easily go places."

Fred had explained to Marcia that his father could trace his ancestry to a Swedish immigrant who homesteaded the ranch during the 1890's. At first, the only requirement for homesteaders to claim their stake was to farm 160 acres for five years. As many settlers moved away from the area during the dry years, the US government raised the allotted acreage to 640, provided it was for a cattle operation. Those changes, along with some good luck, enabled the Bergren family to buy out a number of ranchers on adjoining tracts.

Victor turned the topic to Marcia. "How do you feel about relocating here and being part of our family?"

"I'm a city girl. I grew up in San Francisco. I spent summers at camp and did some horseback riding. That's my only experience with anything remotely like rural life. I love animals. I had a dog, Sandy. He was a Spitz, yellow-brown with a curled up tail. You can tell I don't know much about ranching. I hope Fred's a good teacher."

"What's your family like, Marcia?"

"My dad runs a shipping company – imports and exports to and from Asian countries. Mom free lances as a writer; books and articles for magazines."

"Do you have any brothers or sisters?"

"I have one older sister. She's on a church mission in Uganda."

"What brought you to Droftan University?"

"It's a quality school – and it offered me a full four-year scholarship plus some generous stipends."

"Fred told us about your smarts. I'm glad he met you. He said you coached him over some rough spots."

"How large is your ranch?" Marcia asked.

"About 20,000 acres give or take."

"It must keep you very busy."

"Between the cattle and our wheat, I do stay busy; but I have hired hands to help."

Margaret remained quiet. She was not yet ready to approve Fred's choice, and her stoic demeanor did not go unnoticed by Marcia.

After dinner Fred could sense that Marcia was uncomfortable in his environment, and he wanted to help her feel more at ease. "Let's go into town and have some fun," he suggested.

"I'm all for it."

Later that evening, they drove 22 miles to Crestwood, the nearest town. Its population was 300, and not growing. The music emanating from the community center was unmistakably Western – a guitar, fiddle, banjo, and bass. Fred made his way to the makeshift bar and mixed two glasses of Jack Daniels and Sprite. He and Marcia settled down, sipping their drinks.

"Would you like to dance?"

"Sure. What dance is this?"

"The Texas Two-step."

"I've never danced to it."

"Just follow my lead."

On the way home, Marcia was quiet for the first several minutes. She finally asked, "What other activities are available around here?"

"Many. There's hunting – we have an abundance of game all around. Fishing – the trout are just begging for a line to be dropped. Then, I suppose the highlight of the year is the Fourth of July rodeo. Have you ever been to a rodeo?"

"No. It sounds exciting."

"Politics is a big thing, too, especially local politics, and church activities sometimes. I could teach you to hunt and fish."

68

"Do you think I could learn?"

"Oh yeah."

Marcia lapsed back into silence. She wondered if she could really adjust to this kind of lifestyle; not to mention if she would be able to break down Margaret's opposition.

A few days later the couple headed back to school, delving into their studies and campus life.

*****

Marcia was in a quandary. She loved Fred; his qualities were all she could ever ask for. He was kind, considerate, mature, and intelligent; plus he had those Scandinavian good looks. *But -- and this is a big but -- how could I ever be happy living on that ranch? Fred is an only child, and he will inherit the whole ball of wax someday. I can not expect him to give that up. I need to look at all the ramifications and decide: can I go through with this marriage, or should I break the engagement?*

After days of anguish, Marcia arranged a meeting with Fred. "I'm so sorry to end the engagement, Fred. I want your future to be happy. It would not be, because I would not be happy. I don't know a steer from a bull. And how would my education benefit me out there on the ranch? Our marriage would be doomed to failure. No. My city girl upbringing would be too much for me to overcome there."

"Marcia, it wouldn't need to be that way. We could go away on ski trips. We could take cruises. I would hire a full time maid for you. I know I could make you happy. Won't you reconsider?"

"Fred, you are a wonderful person. Under different circumstances our marriage would be ideal. But in this situation it just wouldn't work. I'm sorry. Here's your ring."

"Marcia, I'm heartbroken."

"So am I, but we must move on."

CHAPTER FOURTEEN

As Marcia's final semester was nearing its end, her career ambitions were still tentative. She had received numerous offers and knew they were based primarily on her academic credentials. She yearned, however, for a challenging job, and kept delaying any acceptance until she could sort out what kind of future she wanted.

Her interest was piqued when a Peace Corps representative visited the campus to recruit volunteers. A personal interview elicited even more interest. She completed the application and other necessary papers, convinced that all follow-up communication would be positive. Suddenly excited, now she was sure she wanted to follow her older sister's footsteps by helping people with great needs. Not only would she satisfy herself, but she would also be pleasing her parents.

When Marcia received a letter from the Peace Corps two weeks later, she was crushed to see that all the vacancies for her choices of assignments had been filled. Only a few open positions remained, and they were in places such as Somalia and Ethiopia.

The drop from euphoria to deep disappointment could not have been more profound. Marcia had really been banking on a Latin American assignment. This was a huge let down.

The next few days were spent in anguish. *I need to look at my options. I need to go back to the Placement Office and see what is available. I'll also have to re-review my offers.* Still, Marcia now felt more focused on her goals; she wanted travel and purposeful work outside the corporate structure.

Marcia talked with Dr. Brazi, her faculty advisor, who made her aware of teaching positions at an elite school in Costa Rica. She read the information in the brochure he had given her. Her interest was generated again, but the one ingredient of helping those in greatest need was missing. *I'm not sure how I would be contributing. Not much sacrifice, either.*

Dr. Brazi showed Marcia testimonials from former teachers: much enjoyment ... satisfaction beyond belief ... great life experience ... friendships for life ... excellent exposure for those wanting to learn more.

"Dr. Brazi, what is your opinion?"

"I think this is a great opportunity. Preparations for staffing are underway now. If you're truly interested, I'll put your name in the pot. Understand that you will be competing against others from throughout the Western Hemisphere."

"Sounds cool. Tell me more."

"Here, let me show you the introduction in the catalog."

Costa Rica, (literally *rich coast,*) is best known for its democratic government and high quality coffee, which is known throughout the world markets. Upwards of 90 percent of its people (called Ticos) over the age of ten are literate. Voting is compulsory for all citizens under 70 years of age. In addition employers, employees, and the government all contribute to a system which provides medical care. Workmen's compensation and social security are other benefits.

Knowing that education is a source of pride for Costa Ricans, a group of foreign wealthy plantation owners there wanted to give something to the country in return for their own success. They formed a consortium to endow a special school. In 1975 the now prestigious Excelente de Escuela (School of Excellence) was established in the city of Katrago. Its elite student body was selected from all the pre-high schools throughout Costa Rica. Faculty members, chosen by a board of governors, were mostly Costa Ricans, but selections of educators from other countries provided the students with diversity and learning enrichment.

Ninety-eight percent of the school's graduates go on to four year colleges; many now occupy positions of prominence both inside and outside the country. The success of the school is recognized throughout the region, but attempts by others to emulate it have not achieved the same results.

"Yes, please nominate me. It sounds exciting."

Dr. Brazi reiterated that the final selection would rest with the Board of Directors of the school. "It just so happens that the representative of the board will be here next Wednesday to conduct interviews. I will make sure you are on the list."

Several weeks later, Marcia received her letter of acceptance to the Excelente de Escuela.

Marcia still had a few doubts. *I'm not absolutely sure this is what I want to do. I need to talk with my parents.* The next day she drove to San Francisco.

Roger and Mary Leed were noted for their wealth and philanthropy. Roger's import-export business dated back three generations. Old money, as the saying goes, meant he was established in stature and power. His active role in the Democratic Party kept his name frequently in the media.

Mary was equally prominent in her own right. Her fame emanated from her expertise in the health field. Earlier, she had served as a public health physician; now she served as a consultant in dietary and related health issues. Her published books and magazine articles were considered to be authoritative in these fields.

Once Marcia arrived at home, she retreated with her parents to the huge library, away from distractions. She displayed the material about Costa Rica and the school, then waited for their response.

Roger spoke first, asking about the Peace Corps. Marcia explained, "I felt that the only choices, which were in Africa, posed too much danger."

Mary agreed wholeheartedly, then asked, "What did your advisor recommend about this school?"

"He gave glowing reports, including testimonials from returning teachers who had gone there."

Roger asked, "Will you be able to master Spanish to the school's satisfaction?"

"Dad, remember I minored in Spanish. And I still have some of my old tapes which I can use to refresh my memory. Best of all, I would be assigned housing with a Costa Rican teacher; I would force myself to converse entirely in their language."

Mary said, "I think this venture will prove to be worthwhile." Marcia, in an apologetic and muted tone, said, "The only hang up I have is the fact that I would not be serving those with the greatest need. Our family has a rich history and tradition of service and sacrifice. I don't want to be the first to change that image."

Roger quickly pointed out that service to others can take many different paths. "Don't feel that you must punish yourself. You will be helping others learn and will no doubt receive a good deal of satisfaction. The greatest teacher ever said, "...the poor will be with us always."

Marcia drove back to campus feeling confident that she had made a good choice.

CHAPTER FIFTEEN

Mai Lois McCoy was now Mai Lois Parker, after being married to Alan Parker for two years. She had met Alan nearly three years ago when she had arranged a trip for him to visit Costa Rica. By that time Mai Lois had made fifteen trips to that country, including some which had involved extended stays to act as guide and interpreter.

Over the years Mai Lois had become very knowledgeable about Costa Rica. Through her exposure to the people and her two semesters of Spanish at UCLA, she had become fluent in the language and able to mix well both with the Ticos and the tour visitors.

Alan had just retired from the FBI office in LA at age 50, and he was exploring the idea of becoming a "pensionata" in Costa Rica. After arriving there he was eager to explore all of its living conditions.

Alan's visit proved to be a worthwhile venture. He and Mai Lois formed a friendship from their week long, one-on-one tour arrangement. They became closer after he invited her out for dinner the last two days. By the end of that week, their friendship in Costa Rica had blossomed into a genuine affection for one another.

Back in Los Angeles, Alan and Mai Lois continued their romance. They had very much in common; both of them had lost their spouses at an early age, and neither had children. Adventure, leisure, and just living life to its fullest were their daily goals. Their compatibility was complete.

Alan's family had a penchant for dabbling in politics. His uncle Horace had never run for public office, but was forever engaged in political campaigns. He was so fervent regarding anything Republican that he often antagonized others who did not share his views. Years ago Horace's belligerent behavior had resulted in the shooting death of his own father, who had been trying to separate Horace from a man with an opposing political position. Uncle Horace never amended his ways.

Alan, returning home from his daily workout at the gym, opened a letter inviting the couple to a barbecue for Senator Edmond Burkhart's reelection.

"Would you like to attend, Mai Lois?"

"I don't think so. I'm not much for politics, but I'll go with you if you want me to."

"Let's go. I'm knowledgeable about some of the issues, and I want to know more about the senator's stand on gun control. There's nothing like first hand exposure to learn a man's real opinions."

There must have been over 300 attending the barbecue. It had, as expected, a very festive atmosphere. The GOP buttons, placards and red, white and blue ribbons were everywhere – on walls, tables, and even the floor. For a hundred dollar donation, attendees could get a necktie with an imprinted elephant.

Senator Burkhart made the rounds, shaking hands and talking with as many people as time would allow. He moved to Alan and they established a rapport that pleased both of them.

"So you're an ex-FBI agent from the LA office?"

"I confess."

"Hey, you're quippy too.

"You must have many contacts and some name recognition in certain circles," the senator opined.

"Yeah, after twelve years in the same place, people did get to know me."

"Are you keeping busy?"

"Not really. I've traveled a lot, but I need to take a break."

"I'll bet you would make a good volunteer for my campaign."

Alan laughed. "How do you know we are together on your agenda?"

"How could you not be?"

"I'm giving you a rough time. Let me think about it."

"Your thoughts just meshed with my objective. You're smart, perceptive and have presence. How 'bout it?"

"Okay! Give me some general guidelines, and I'm ready to work."

A few days later Alan met again with Senator Burkhart. Later he was indoctrinated on the ins and outs of campaigning. He hadn't realized there was so much grunt work, such as mailing brochures, writing letters and placing advertising, but he delved into these tasks with zeal.

Weeks passed and the election was close at hand. Senator Burkhart's opponent, Mark Dyer, was a popular career politician with heavy funding. The state of California had more registered Democrats than Republicans, which made it an uphill battle. When the results were counted, it was Dyer 50.5% and Burkhart 49.5%.

It had been a contentious battle for the senate seat, but one which was clean and without the usual mudslinging. Senator Burkhart offered his congratulations. Now he was uncertain about his future, but not ready to retire.

The Republicans regained the White House and several key senate seats, giving them a majority in that chamber.

A few months later ex-senator Edmund Burkhart was notified by Kenneth Bennett, the President's Chief of Staff, that the President wanted to favor him with an Ambassadorship. The ex-senator was elated. "You've been a party faithful, voting along party lines nearly all the time. We don't forget you when you get voted out of office."

Mr. Bennett made no mention of which countries were available. It did not matter. Alan Parker immediately came to mind when his thoughts were directed to staffing the new office.

"Hey! Let's get together. I have some important matters I want to discuss with you," Burkhart e-mailed to Alan.

In the meantime, the White House staff told him that he could choose among the following postings: Algeria, Panama, Poland, or Costa Rica. He and Alan met with two other campaign workers the next day. When advised of the choices, Alan strongly suggested Costa Rica. After some discussion, among the group it was settled – Costa Rica.

Alan, Mai Lois, and two others attended the swearing in ceremony. It was during this event that Edmund Burkhart met Mai Lois and became aware of her vast knowledge of the country and her travel experiences. At the prompting of Alan, she made an effort to associate herself with the embassy staff. Recognizing her value, Mr. Burkhart easily found a place for her. She would be acting as an agenda developer and travel liaison between the staff and the Costa Ricans.

The Costa Rica decision had Mai Lois' memory retracing to the time many years ago when she had met a handsome, young engineer. She remembered his name and the prediction he had made about her finding "Mr. Right." Yes, Jeff Benson had spoken with conviction. She hadn't put much credence in what he said at the time, but now how accurate it was. His prediction had come true.

The changeover from the existing embassy staff was orderly and cooperative, taking only about ten days. The initial duties of the new staff mostly involved protocol and entertaining and visiting with Costa Rican government officials.

*****

Marcia Leed arrived at Katrago in April, the end of the dry season. At the airport terminal, she stepped outside to meet a van arranged by the school. Before boarding she looked around and took a deep breath. *Ah, that cool breeze is so refreshing.* The thermometer at the airport bank read 78 degrees. She knew that Katrago, a city in a country near the equator, owes its comfort to its elevation over 4000 feet above sea level.

The fifteen mile drive to the school gave her a good glimpse of the city. The approach to the school campus was a landscaper's dream achievement. Huge royal poincianas, some with blooms of bright red and others with bright orange, towered above the lower growing ginger plants. The campus was laid out in a formal design with vistas partitioned off to provide visual breaks from the vast acreage.

"Buenas tardes. Me llama Anita Morales."

Marcia, surprised by an unexpected voice coming from behind her, replied, *"Me llama Marcia Leed,"* as she turned to face a young lady with the tone in her voice asking acceptance, yet not the least bit submissive. Anita's eyes sparkled when she smiled, showing natural affection. Marcia saw that the girl was about two inches shorter than herself, but by no means was she short. Her complexion was flawless, and not as dark as most Latinas.

"Let me show you your new home."

As they walked Anita explained that she had arrived a day earlier and had become familiar with the school and the housing. She showed Marcia a garden apartment with a group of six others, about a quarter mile from the larger apartment complex. It was a stand-alone two bedroom unit, complete with a small kitchen and living room.

"Oh, this is lovely," Marcia said as she walked around looking at the furnishings.

Anita's body language said it all: in the short time they had been together, Marcia could see that here was a happy, feisty, and outgoing girl.

"Here is our schedule for tomorrow," Anita offered. "Looks like a busy day ahead of us."

Marcia looked at the printout of their schedule for the next two weeks. The first week consisted of visits to various points of interest throughout the country. The itinerary included, on page two, a meet and greet and a get-acquainted party at the US Embassy in San Jose.

Marcia and seven other American teachers from the Excelente de Escuela attended, along with a group of American ex-patriots. The embassy wanted them to know they had a source of assistance if and whenever needed.

Ambassador Burkhart presented a brief rundown on relations between Costa Rica and the American government. Next was a speech about some of the "do's and don'ts" by Mai Lois. During the Happy Hour that followed, Mai Lois and Marcia spent a few minutes chatting with each other about several mundane topics.

The second week's schedule was an orientation of the school.

Classes began in mid-May, with Anita teaching history and geography, while Marcia was teaching math and computer science.

Marcia had remembered that in her own high school days not all the students had a desire to learn. In fact, disruptions had been frequent. Here, however, she saw that most of the kids were disciplined and courteous. Classes were small, allowing for individual direction. The structured lesson plans simplified the teaching, allowing freedom for personal one-on-one time.

Outside of the classroom socializing with Anita was most friendly. However, Anita's brash and effervescent manner at times conflicted with Marcia's more proper ways. Too often, she teased Marcia for being too prudish.

The first semester ended with over 80 percent of the students in Marcia's class attaining top grades. Follow-up achievement tests reinforced the accuracy of the grading.

*****

The break between semesters gave both girls a stress free two week reprieve from the classroom.

"How would you like seeing more of the country? I can give you a first class tour. Would a Cobra suit your fancy? My family owns an automobile agency, and I have unlimited liberties with our cars."

The trip to San Jose the next day offered a chance for Marcia to meet Anita's family. It wasn't eventful, since her mother was away and her father was busy dealing with disgruntled customers. He greeted the girls hurriedly, then went about his business. Anita summoned a crew to prep the car, and they were ready to hit the road.

The girls first traveled over 150 miles to the *Riu Juanacaste Hotel* located on the beautiful Matapalo Beach near Liberia. They arrived mid afternoon, which gave them plenty of time for swimming and snorkeling. They discovered later why the resort was famous for its entertainment and international cuisine.

Early the next day they traveled to the ancient city of Quartiago to stop at the Cathedral de Marie Velope, where Anita drank the holy water to receive a blessing. Marcia was somewhat indifferent to the ritual but participated anyway. Later that afternoon they did some shopping for jeans and party dresses.

Marcia and Anita were both eager for the night life when they returned to the resort. During dinner, a Latin band performed. The two were seated at a table close to the dance floor. Two men took a table nearby. Not unnoticed by Marcia, Anita gave them prolonged eye contact. One came over and announced, "*Me llama* Oskar Van Nostrand. May I have the pleasure of dancing with ...?"

"*Me llama* Anita. Yes, the band is playing a cha-cha. It's my favorite."

Returning to the table, Oskar asked Marcia if his companion could join them. "Yes, it is okay. Who is your friend?" Franz Hoff walked over and introduced himself.

Franz was the taller and more handsome of the two; more congenial, too. "We have a Latino club back home in Holland, but the music is not as good as here."

Anita spoke up, "I thought your names sounded Dutch, but I wasn't sure. What brings you here?"

Oskar replied, "We're both botanists. We work for a bulb and seed company in Holland. Our work is mostly hybridizing plants. We have a challenge now trying to develop tuberous begonias that will be able to withstand hot summers."

As the night wore on the couples became more friendly and began to dance closer.

The girls excused themselves to go to the restroom together. Inside, Anita said, 'Oskar and Franz want to spend the night with us."

"Huh! No way!"

Marcia, you need to let your hair down. Have some fun. These guys are first class. It will be great. I know it will."

"Anita, you don't know them."

"Why do we need to know them?"

"You've had too much to drink."

"Two martinis – same as you."

"Count me out."

Several dances later, Oskar and Anita returned to their table. Anita was preparing to sit when Oskar lifted her hand and led her out of the room. She looked back over her shoulder. "Sure you don't want to come?"

"I'm sure." Marcia did not want to follow them but did not want to stay, either. After some contemplation she left with Franz following a few paces behind.

When she and Franz entered the girls' room, Anita and Oskar were exchanging kisses and were well on their way to escalate their love. Much to the surprise and enjoyment of Oskar, Anita began undressing and exhibiting herself in different poses. "If you've never seen a nude model pose, take a good look."

Oskar's anxiety could not be held in check. He grabbed Anita and gently pushed her onto to bed. A scene of unbridled action punctuated with unintelligible utterances ensued.

Franz moved over to Marcia, planting light kisses. She first resisted, but as the kisses became more lasting, she yielded. The scene across the room intensified her libido. The urge was just too strong; her inhibitions completely left her. Marcia joined fully into the fray.

When the two girls awoke late the next morning, the men had already left. A leisurely morning awaited them and they both welcomed it.

"Didn't I tell you we would have a great time, Marcia?"

"Yeah, but I much prefer to know who I bed down with."

Laughing, Anita teased, "Marcia, do you think that holy water was spiked?"

"That's not funny."

CHAPTER SIXTEEN

E rnesto (Che) Alvarez was born in a small village just outside Managua, the capital city of Nicaragua. During his formative years he witnessed an unstable government and widespread corruption – a classic situation of the haves and have-nots.

The choice for Ernesto was clear cut. Poor, uneducated and with no way to see a better future, he sided with the Sandinistas, a Socialist movement headed by Daniel Ortega. The Contras, in power with the aid of the US government, had an overwhelming advantage with weapons and money. The funds they received were funneled from secret sales to Iran for prisoner releases. This setup became known as the Iran-Contra Affair. The US Congress had earlier denied funding, but the CIA's covert operations prevailed.

Ernesto proudly accepted his position as a Sandinista soldier as soon as he reached the age of sixteen. He considered himself to be a revolutionary hero, taking the name Che in honor of his role model, Che Guevara, a socialist and best friend of Fidel

Castro, who was noted for his expertise in helping to overthrow governments.

After several years the revolution in Nicaragua ended when both sides declared a truce of sorts. Daniel Ortega was allowed to step down in peace from his leadership, and the US Congress stopped all aid.

Young Ernesto was falsely accused of murder when a witness misidentified him in a police lineup. He was serving a life sentence in prison when he escaped during a work detail. Slipping across the border into Costa Rica, he settled in the province of Guancaste in the northwestern area of the country bordering Nicaragua.

Ernesto's life was not better there, eking out a living as a plantation laborer. When that kind of work became scarce, he found odd jobs around the area, working in hotels and restaurants. He eventually teamed up with a fellow laborer, Antonio (Tony) Sanchez. The two men's lives were improved when they began to steal money and belongings from hotel guests, mostly on the beach and around swimming pools. Soon they had accumulated enough money to purchase a used truck.

*****

On the third morning of their visit to the resort, Marcia and Anita found themselves sightseeing along the coast, stopping to visit fishing villages and to view luxury hotels. En route to the Santa Rosa National Park, they observed lush foliage, rich with color. The Arenal Volcano was visible in the distance when they entered the Central Highland. This day of relaxation was capped off with a folklore night show at Pueble Anteguo.

The beach adjacent to their hotel was a strand of unspoiled sugar-white sand about a mile long, which curved into a lagoon before reaching layered rock formations. The girls overheard other guests talking about having hiked along the shore to the rocks, which was a favorite picnic spot. The sedimentary rocks were mostly flat. Smoothed by centuries of wind, rain, and surf, they were ideal for tables and seats.

The next day was sunny and pleasant when Marcia and Anita started their hike to the rocks. They were diverted from their goal about a half mile along the beach where they spotted a tiki hut and heard a noisy crowd dancing to island music.

Anita said, "Hey! This is what it's all about! Come on! Let's join in the fun!" They somehow found an empty table and ordered margaritas. Several couples were on the dance floor, gyrating their hips and grooving to the music. Not surprisingly, Anita joined in. Marcia was content to sit it out.

Unaware that two strangers were observing their every move, the girls sipped their margaritas and clapped their hands to the beat.

When the band quit playing, Marcia and Anita continued on their way to see the rocks they had been hearing so much about. When they reached the slightly elevated formations, they stood silently enjoying the panoramic view of the beach and the sea. Soon the sun retreated behind clouds, and at the same time they noticed that the beach was almost deserted. "We should head back to the hotel," Marcia said.

Two men suddenly appeared. The one closest to the girls approached with a faint smile, as though he were going to ask for directions. Suddenly, he grabbed Anita by the arm. "Don't panic. I have a knife under my shirt. I won't hurt you unless you try to run away," Che said.

Tony held a knife to Marcia. Panicked, she screamed, "What do you want from us?"

"Ransom money. We want *yanqui* ransom money. You owe us; you gave aid to our enemy."

Both men reeked of several days of perspiration, not to mention the odors they had picked up from handling garbage.

"Anita. What's going on? How did they know I was an American?"

"We heard you talking at the hotel. We saw your Cobra, too, so we know you have money. We followed you here."

"Where are you taking us?"

"Just be quiet." The men pushed the girls around the rocks to a dirt road, where they had parked an old truck out of view. "Get in the truck."

Soon the girls were bound and forced into the old Toyota pickup which had been covered with a makeshift canopy.

Che drove the truck along the road about ten miles, eventually turning onto the highway. When they came to a truck stop, he pulled over, jumped out of the vehicle and went inside to purchase some junk food and two ten liter carboys of purified water, using money he had stolen from the girls. He put his purchases in the back of the truck, locked the girls' purses in the glove compartment, and ordered Marcia to get out. Then he led her to a telephone booth.

"Call the American Embassy in San Jose," he ordered. "Speak only in Spanish so I can understand you. Tell them who you are and that you are captured. To free you they must send us ten million colon (about $20,000). Details will come later."

Marcia got through to the embassy after some difficulty. Mai Lois answered the call. She asked for their location, and Marcia responded in English; only to be abruptly cut off by Che.

Che forced her back onto the bed of the pickup, then drove them down the highway and onto a circular lane. He parked the truck, ordered the girls to get out, then said, "We will go up this cliff."

Tony could carry only one carboy and still be in full control of the captives. The path was steep, zigzagging almost horizontally. When all four reached the top they were exhausted and needed to rest. The captors had picked a heavily wooded and isolated spot.

"Do you think they will let us go when they get the ransom?" Marcia asked, speaking in English so the men would not understand her.

"No. These men are criminals. Expect the worst."

"What do you mean?"

"I mean our lives are at stake, Marcia. We know their names. We could identify them. They will not want to leave any evidence behind."

Marcia was frightened, and she looked to Anita for advice. "Do something. Outsmart them!"

Anita responded, "This is a desperate situation, and it calls for desperate action. We've got to be bold. Here's the plan." She described it in hushed tones, speaking in English.

Che sent Tony back down the cliff to retrieve the other carboy of water. As soon as she was sure he must be almost all the way to the bottom, Anita called out, "I need to pee!"

"You can pee when I take you out to the shack where your home will be for the next few days." Anita could see the wood and tarpaper structure, which was about ten feet square with no windows. Wide cracks had been left between the boards for ventilation. She knew she did not want to be left alone in there.

"No! I can't wait! I'm hurting!"

Che untied her wrists with a warning. "Don't try anything you will regret. Else you will never see your friend alive again."

Anita walked a few yards into a thicket and pretended to pee. She returned and stepped close to Che holding out her hands to be retied. As he fumbled with the stiff rope, she backed slowly toward the edge of the cliff. He followed her. While he was looking down, she kicked him in the crotch as hard as she could. He groped, bent over, and dropped his knife. When Anita gave him one more kick right on the bulls eye, Marcia was able to ram him with her body even though her hands were still tied. Taking advantage of Che's pain, the two girls scuffled with him until, with one big coordinated push, they tumbled him over the edge. They saw him fall until he was caught in some underbrush about half-way down.

A few moments later, Tony reappeared lugging the second carboy. When he saw both girls untied and Anita wielding a knife, the now leaderless thug froze, then fled noisily out of sight.

*****

After she received the telephone call, Mai Lois had immediately notified Alan. Checking the embassy caller ID they pinpointed the location of the truck stop pay phone. Not wanting to put out an alarm for fear of some yet unknown repercussions, the two headed for the truck stop.

Free and relieved, Marcia and Anita descended the cliff as quickly as they could. They managed to hike back to the highway, where they flagged down a passing tour bus. They asked to be dropped off at the same truck stop where Marcia had made the call. As the girls got off the bus, they were met by Alan and Mai Lois.

Several days later, after learning the details of his daughter's harrowing experience, Roger Leed remarked to his wife, Mary. "I'm hard pressed to understand how certain events happen. Marcia refused a Peace Corps assignment in Africa because she thought it would be too dangerous. How ironic."

PART THREE

CHAPTER SEVENTEEN

The symptoms of Jeff Benson's psychosomatic illness had lingered for almost a year. The hypnosis sessions with Dr. Zachery had lessened the frequency of his sudden outbreaks; however, the melancholy persisted. Rex could see Jeff's work quality diminishing and suggested he take time off. "Relax. Walk in the park. Stroll along the beach." But when Rex suggested that Jeff visit his brother in Seattle, Jeff nixed that idea right off. He did not want his brother to see him in his present mental and physical condition.

*****

The income and expense statements for Stewart Brothers Architects and Engineers, as shown by the last audit, were not yielding a satisfactory level of profit. Rex Newton, never one to accept even a temporary downturn in the partnership, determined to learn the underlying causes of the problem so he could take corrective measures. He had attended an efficiency workshop several months earlier and had been impressed with the leader's presentation. He found Beverly Appleton's business card, and soon he and Jeff met with her for a brief orientation.

Both partners were pleased with her suggestions, and they entered in a contract with Beverly's firm

Beverly arrived at the office a few days later. She and her clerk, Dexter, met with Jeff. She requested and was given a vast array of income and expense information. It was during a meeting the next day that she noticed a tic interrupting Jeff's conversation.

Rex's wife Becky arrived on the scene. "Beverly, how is the project coming along?"

"Dexter and I should wrap up the on-site part with two more sessions."

"Did you receive everything you needed?"

"Everything. Jeff had all the materials in A-one shape."

"You look a little puzzled, though. Is something bothering you?"

Looking around to be sure Jeff had left the room, Beverly moved closer to Becky and asked in muted tones "... is Jeff an epileptic?"

"I'm glad you asked. No, he's had some serious problems over the death of his wife."

"So, his problem is not genetic?"

"No, it's temporary. I wouldn't let it bother you; his doctor has high hopes for his complete recovery. By the way, Rex and I are having Jeff over for dinner this evening. Why don't you join us?"

"Well ..."

"I've been cooking on and off for Jeff recently. He has already accepted my invitation. One more will make the evening more like a party. Please do come. Maybe a bit early – say, six – and we'll have our own happy hour."

The dinner party allowed Jeff and Beverly to become more at ease with one another. The two highballs for Jeff apparently helped to put him at ease; there were no tics or outbursts. He saw more than good looks in Beverly. Her quick wit and hearty laugh belied her stern working habits.

The last on-site audit provided Jeff with another opportunity to be with Beverly. Even though it was a business meeting, he took advantage of the time and asked her for a beach walk. Beverly realized that it was not an appropriate request and refused in a polite tone. She explained that such a get together between herself and a client was not a good idea, and not in accordance with her firm's practices. She sensed that he was a bit upset. She turned from him, closed her eyes, and faced a blank wall. *What if I unwittingly cause his illness to worsen?* Turning back, she added, "Maybe I've been too hasty. Would tomorrow afternoon suit you?"

The ensuing stroll had all the earmarks of a beginning friendship – but only if Jeff could feel it. When they held hands, there was simply no magnetism. Near the end of their walk, they approached a pier that jutted from far inland to far out into the water. Underneath was a wide shade formed by massive timbers. Beverly allowed herself to be tugged under the pier and held tightly. Jeff planted a kiss on her neck. She faced him directly and looked into his eyes. Her blue eyes were bright even in the dark shadows. Her full lips invited the next step. Jeff wanted to test his feelings. They kissed. Then Jeff looked away. *Where's my affection? I've lost my mojo!*

"Is there something wrong?"

"No, I just wasn't sure you would be receptive."

"Well, maybe it's time we got back to the car."

Two weeks later Beverly delivered her final report. Jeff gave the paper a cursory look, then offered, "Let me treat you to lunch at that new place on Bradberry Drive."

"Okay."

During lunch, Beverly could see Jeff's disappointment. "Tell me all about your troubles," she invited.

"Yesterday I attended the Rock of Ages Church where my wife and I were married. Several days ago I had sent a generous donation and a check for flowers to be placed in front of the pulpit to honor the one year anniversary of her death. I'm upset. No mention of the flowers at any time, nor in the church bulletin. Now I want to learn first hand what went wrong. Would you mind if we went there before I drop you off at your home?"

"No, I'm in no hurry."

The church was not far from the restaurant. In a few minutes they met with Roy Barron, an assistant pastor responsible for the altar flowers. Jeff explained how he had expected recognition but had not been given any.

"Could you correct the mistake next Sunday?"

"Are you a member here?"

"No."

"Then you will not receive recognition."

"Is that a church policy?"

"No, it's my policy."

"Then you can keep my checks and stuff your selfish rule."

The pastor added calmly, "If you and your girlfriend are living together, you are living in sin."

Jeff stood up. "What is wrong with you?"

Beverly grabbed Jeff by the arm. "Let's get out of here."

When Jeff arrived home later that afternoon, he remembered receiving mail solicitations from the church and went directly to a drawer in his business bureau. Opening it, he was filled with disbelief when he found fifty two small envelopes – one for each week's offering– interspersed with several other small envelopes intended for special giving. *I think I will set aside a time for a small ceremony ... and I will destroy these envelopes.*

Jeff couldn't sleep that night. He got out of bed, poured himself a double shot of bourbon, and stepped out onto his lanai. Looking toward the back yard, he felt a gentle breeze. When it subsided, he heard a dog bark in the distance. A siren from an emergency vehicle wailed, then was quiet. He looked up at a bright starry sky and spoke out loud: "What a hell of a day! Has some demon come into my life? How much more can I suffer? I'm a wreck."

He turned to go back inside. *I remember what Coach Yeary said many times: "When the going gets tough, the tough get going." I've just got to hang on and tough this thing out.*

PART FOUR

CHAPTER EIGHTEEN

S EVERAL YEARS EARLIER ...

In this flat, arid, West Texas Permian basin, pump jacks no longer lay dormant. Production had been declining over the last several decades as significant amounts of crude oil were tapped out. Recently, however, a godsend had been bestowed on the folks here thanks to new technologies such as hydraulic fracturing. Word about this new level of activity generated excitement throughout the area.

*****

George Schaggs left his job as a handyman on a cattle ranch to become a roustabout in the oil fields. His new work included a good deal of wildcatting, which required him to move from place to place.

After finishing a two week work schedule, George returned home to his family. His three children heard the old Ford F-150 pickup rounding the corner and heading down the dead-end dirt road to their house. Their excitement erupted into a clamoring noise because they knew there was a treat awaiting them.

George parked between another pickup and a rusted out Plymouth which had long since become a relic. As he entered the house the kids converged on him, tugging at his legs and competing for attention. They were eager to tell him their choice for supper ... this day it would be McDonald's.

Before the family could get started on the two mile trip to town, George asked, "Where's your mama?"

Blanche, the oldest of the three children at fifteen, yelled above the rattle of the window air conditioning unit, "I don't know. She left for work about a week ago. We haven't seen her since."

Velma worked as a waitress at the local Busy Bee Cafe. She had often been away from home for a day or two at a time, but never this long before.

George growled. "I'm not surprised. She was worthless from day one. I should've kicked her ass out a long time ago. I've heard talk about her and that Carl Sparks. He's a loser, too. Let'er have her fun. We'll be better off if she stays with that no good son of a bitch."

The next day George, seated in his dirty, ragged recliner, gathered all three of the kids in a tight circle on the floor so he could explain the changes in their future. Without any prompting, Blanch walked over to the fridge, grabbed a Bud Light, and handed it to her dad.

He lifted the tab and took a big swallow. "Problems, problems. Hell, I've got more problems than Dick Tracy." He pulled out a pack of Marlboros from his shirt pocket. Before he lit up he hesitated, then said the words his kids expected. "I don't have a housekeeper ready to take care of y'all and look after the place. Blanche, honey, you'll have to take over 'til I can find somebody."

"Do you want me to stay in school?"

"Yeah. And I want you to graduate."

Late Sunday night George left the house to travel to his next job.

Having the responsibility for the house and kids made Blanche feel even more needed, although it drained her by the end of the day. She made sure that the two younger ones – Butch, ten, and Cathy, eight – were fed, properly clothed, and that they each carried out their own tasks.

All was not drudgery. Blanche looked forward to grocery shopping, because it provided her an opportunity to purchase the *National Enquirer, The Globe*, and other tabloids. From an early age she had envisioned becoming a movie star. All the Hollywood gossip, dirt, glamor and love triangles played into her interests and desires. She read the tabloids with a burning intensity.

When she reached sixteen, Blanche looked more like a young woman than a girl, and a pretty one at that. Her appearance did not go unnoticed. Offers of dates were numerous, and she didn't refuse very many. The typical date included a movie and later a drive to a secluded place. It was not long before she had gained the reputation of being promiscuous. That kind of news traveled fast and became a source of embarrassment, both to her and to her siblings. Her life began to unravel. She had consistently ranked near the top of her class, but now her grades began to slip badly. The inevitable happened. Blanche dropped out of school before she finished the eleventh grade.

George, anxious to find someone to help with his kids, found a woman at a roadside tavern. It didn't matter to him that she came with her own baggage; a boy, seven, and a girl, five. Joyce jumped at the chance to get settled in a house, since she had been living in a rented unit at a fleabag motel. With little concern for George's children, she moved in and immediately claimed rights and privileges. Her children and the Schaggs family were suddenly thrown into pandemonium. The Brady Bunch it was not.

*****

Blanche had found work at the Playland Bowling Alley snack bar, and she stayed away from home as much as possible, returning only to sleep and have an occasional meal. She worked hard – this was her first real job, and she wanted to keep it.

On the day Blanche turned seventeen, she held up a hand mirror. Peering into it, she recited an old poem:

"Mirror, mirror in my hand

Who is the fairest in the land?"

She kept looking at herself, admiring her violet eyes and her thick, shiny black hair. Blanche laid the mirror down and with delicate touches began to caress her body. *Nature has been kind to me – even generous. I'll never need breast implants, and I'm tall even without having to wear spike heels. Most glamorous movie stars would envy my beauty. And my body – it always gets a second look.*

Picking up the mirror again to take a last look, Blanche smiled. Her crooked teeth were her only flaw; a flaw she was determined to correct. *I won't let my teeth hold me back. I promise.*

Several weeks later Blanche arranged for a sub at the bowling alley and took the afternoon off. Armed with torn out yellow pages from the phone book, she drove her dad's other pickup truck to Central City, parking on a side street.

The first listing under "orthodontists" was located two blocks down the street. A small stand-alone building, it stood between residential condominiums. Blanche went in and asked the receptionist for an appointment. The woman silently handed her several pages of forms to complete, gave her a pen, and pointed to a chair.

When she was sure nobody was watching, Blanche slipped down the hall, trying to catch a glimpse of the orthodontist. She was suddenly challenged by the receptionist and told she was where she did not belong. "I'm looking for the restroom," she lied.

"Down that hall."

On her way, Blanche looked into each room she passed. She finally saw a bespectacled elderly man with stooped shoulders slowly making his way between a patient and a medicine cabinet. She immediately exited the premises, dumping the forms into a nearby receptacle.

Undeterred, Blanche returned to the truck and looked up the next office on the page. It was located in a strip shopping center not too far away. Following the same routine, she was able to catch a glimpse of a fortyish man wearing a white lab coat. She reasoned that he must be the orthodontist.

In completing the forms, Blanche fudged several details so she would appear to have a respectable home environment. She wrote that her mother was a teacher and her father an accountant. She inflated her salary from the bowling alley, as well.

A few days later, the treatments began on her teeth as planned. Blanche had saved enough from her salary – and from whatever she could skim from her job receipts – to make the initial payment of $800. However, on her second appointment the head office clerk demanded a second payment of a like amount.

Blanche informed Dr. Reynolds about her plight, and asked for a private meeting. Soon the two of them were face-to-face in his office.

"Dr. Reynolds, I have a problem. I don't have any more money, but maybe we can somehow work out an arrangement so I can complete my treatments?"

"What did you have in mind?"

At that moment, Blanche slowly crossed her legs, allowing her skirt to inch up well above her knees. She smiled, then said,

"Are you so engrossed in your practice that you don't have time for more pleasant activities?"

"If I read you correctly, the answer is no – an emphatic no! I'm busy, I'm not interested, and besides I'm a married man. I don't want to tarnish my good reputation."

"You won't, because only the two of us will ever know. I can give you pleasure like you've never had before." Blanche looked up at the doctor through her eyelashes. "It would be an opportunity for you that could never be repeated. Think about it. I'll be back on Saturday at two o'clock. That is your day off, isn't it?"

Blanche had noticed how fidgety Dr. Reynolds had been when she displayed her assets and acted in a provocative way. That assured her that he was not immune to temptation, and gave her encouragement to carry out her plan.

The following Saturday at exactly two o'clock Blanche arrived at the orthodontist's office. The door was locked, and for a moment she wondered if the doc had gotten cold feet. She rattled the door and was pleased to hear footsteps. As he opened the door, Dr. Reynolds smiled and tried to appear calm. After a few pleasantries were exchanged, he suggested they play first and work later. She agreed.

This liaison continued for months, until the dental work was finished and Blanche's teeth were in perfect alignment. At the end of the last meeting, she announced, "I want my $800 back."

"What? Are you crazy? You got what you wanted, and so did I. The game is over. Now go away, and get lost."

"You don't understand. I want my $800 back," Blanche repeated.

"No way. Now go!"

"Do you want me to tell all?"

"Who would believe you? It would be your word against mine, and there are no witnesses."

"Your sperm is on a pair of my panties. I'm sure you've heard of DNA testing?"

There were a few moments of silence. Then Dr. Reynolds spoke quietly. "I don't keep cash here."

"No problem. There's an ATM at the bank on the corner. I'll wait here for you."

The orthodontist soon returned. "Take this money, you evil slut. I never want to see you again."

"You won't," Blanche promised. And she left.

CHAPTER NINETEEN

The leagues at the Playland Bowling Alley were each composed of a different segment of the surrounding communities. One of the team bowlers in the league from nearby Barker Air Force Base took a shine to Blanche. They began dating and their frequent encounters developed into a serious relationship. He was 23 and into his second enlistment, holding the rank of Staff Sergeant.

Howard Bowman had never intended to be in the military, much less in a second hitch. Before enlisting he had almost completed two years of study in speech and dramatics at St. Benedict College in Minnesota when his dad, a diabetic, became gravely ill. Funds that had been designated for college had to be diverted to cover his dad's medical expenses. Howard heard about monetary assistance from the military, available for education after completing an enlistment. He joined only for this reason.

Based on his occupational testing and career guidance, he was assigned to training in intelligence. This choice proved to be a field he enjoyed; thus he decided to make the Air Force his career.

When Howard proposed marriage, Blanche readily accepted and quit her job. She looked at the upcoming marriage as an escape from the turmoil at home as well as an opportunity to fulfill her own ambitions.

The wedding ceremony was held at the base chapel. It was simple and attended by only a few friends. The chaplain conducted the entire affair in less than thirty minutes.

After a short honeymoon to El Paso and Juarez, Mexico, the young couple settled in a rented apartment off base.

Now was the golden opportunity Blanche had been anticipating – a name change. She detested her names, first, last, and every damn blasted syllable. The change was more than merely becoming Mrs. Bowman. *What better time to go all out? I will henceforth be known as Clara Bowman.* The name was a nod to Clara Bow, the "It" girl, who was one of Blanche's favorite movie stars from the early screen era.

Howard was pleased beyond any measure to have latched onto a beautiful girl who also excelled at domestic work. The two of them enjoyed many happy times together.

Clara could have had a considerable amount of free time, but she was not one to sit around. First, she tackled getting her GED, or high school equivalency diploma. She managed this with no difficulty. Then she learned of a degreed program offered at the local Seaton Community College for paralegal certification. This was a great opportunity, and she did not want to pass it up. In a short time that degree was added to her accomplishments.

Clara interviewed with the visiting recruiters who were seeking graduates in the legal field. Several represented firms too far away, but when Brady and Horvath, a firm located in Midland, extended an offer, she readily accepted. Once at work, her aggressiveness and "can do" attitude won accolades and helped her bridge the gap between being just a novice to being a progressive, seasoned and valuable employee.

During this period she and Howard began to entertain, party, and engage themselves in local affairs. They attended numerous plays, operas and other theatrical productions. Howard's education and previous exposure to the arts enabled him to be an expert mentor for Clara. She eagerly incorporated all this knowledge, using it to her advantage as she strove to become a respected member of their community.

After they had attended "My Fair Lady," at the local theater, Howard remarked how Clara's background was so similar to that of Eliza Doolittle.

"Yes, you're right. But do not belittle me."

"No, I'm not doing that. I just want to see you in a better light."

"My home life was similar, but don't expect me to recite all that jazz about the rain in Spain. And, if I hear one more word about the way I spread my legs when I sit down, or the giggle in my laugh, or the way I hold my fork, I'll scream to high heaven."

"Clara, you have all the qualities it takes to become a refined lady. I know I'm too critical at times, but it's for your own good. Try to understand."

"I'll try."

*****

Not long afterwards. Howard received orders for an overseas transfer to the Military Assistance Advisory Group (MAAG) at the American Embassy in Brussels, Belgium. Once there, he moved into lodging provided for him in a downtown Brussels hotel. About two months later the military arranged for Clara to join him.

When a vacancy for a legal assistant in the nearby Staff Judge Advocate's Office opened up, Clara applied for the position and was accepted. It was a small office, with just one officer, a Major Stowe, and one assistant.

The job turned out to be a real plum. Clara and Howard found time to take trips to Paris, Vienna and other European capitals. Truly, a fantasy world had opened up for them.

After returning from a performance at the Mozart Music Festival in Vienna, Clara and Howard were enjoying a quiet evening together on their hotel balcony. The conversation drifted to their future plans; what they would be doing after they relocated back to the United States.

Howard reminisced about how he and his brother enjoyed the opportunities their father had provided for them. He asked Clara, "What are your feelings about starting a family?"

"A family just does not fit into my plans at all, Howard. I had to care for a younger brother and sister, and that deprived me of a normal childhood. No, I'm not ready for kids now – maybe never."

Howard said quietly, "I want a son or two. I want to take them fishing and camping; I want to help them with their homework; I want to watch them play ball. Don't you want a daughter you could idolize?"

"No, Howard. I'm sorry. You've got the wrong person."

Howard said, "Clara, I don't beg easily, but I'm begging you now. I want children. What would it take to make you change your mind?"

"Nothing. I would rather we just drop the subject."

"You don't know what children would mean to me. It's very important. Why? Why can't you see it my way? What could possibly be more important for you?"

"I want recognition. I want a future, prestige. I want wealth. I want all the things I don't have now."

"Either we've changed or I really have married the wrong person."

"Perhaps some of both, Howard. It's getting late. We'll look at everything in a different way tomorrow."

Howard agonized over their conversation all through the next day. When he could no longer keep his frustration bottled up, he initiated a follow up session with Clara.

"We've got to come to grips with this problem. Our marriage is at stake."

Clara said, "I've had six years of a good life, and I hope you've had the same."

"Have you always been true?"

"Howard, I'll say it once more. I'm ambitious."

"Meaning?"

"Meaning that I'm willing to go to great lengths to achieve my objectives."

"Such as?"

"How do you think I got that promotion and all those glowing performance evaluations from Major Stowe?"

Howard was silent for a long moment. "I trusted you, but now I think it's time for us to move on separately."

"I was hoping you would be the one to initiate that suggestion."

Clara's transformation from a girl with a lack of social graces and verbal skills to one who could find her way in a wide range of situations filled her with eager anticipation for her future. The past appeared to have led her step-by-step to a high level of confidence. Now she knew what to do and what to expect. *Do I have a supernatural being with traits like myself guiding me? Regardless, I am ready and eager to face the future. I am driven!*

CHAPTER TWENTY

After leaving Costa Rica, Marcia Leed had worked for three years as a software engineer at Xtreme Technics in Silicon Valley. The job was ideal, with a good working environment and juicy perks – library, gym time, and social clubs.

Xtreme Technics, like other software firms, was caught in competition and was forced to downsize. Marcia managed to escape the first staff reduction and held on to her position for awhile. More cut backs came later, however, and she received the dreaded pink slip.

Marcia felt her skills were marketable, and she did not want to rush into a job search. She took a short ski trip to Aspen, followed by a visit to her parents in San Francisco. She had dated on and off – but nothing serious, so there was no compelling reason to remain in the area. She was free to relocate if necessary.

The days of idleness were beginning to become boring. She needed friendship and decided to call her former college roommate.

"Hello, Susan. This is Marcia. What's going on down there in LA?"

"I've been really busy. You know. Tax season and all. What about you?"

"I'm unemployed. Not really looking. But I'll need to get with it before too long."

"Plenty of jobs here. Why don't you come down and see what might interest you?"

"Do you mean it?"

"Of course. I can bed you down for awhile."

"I'll take you up on that. Should be there in three or four days. I'll call you again before I leave."

Susan Maddox was a CPA sharing a two bedroom apartment with Angela Fieldman, an employment placement specialist.

Marcia was eager to make the trip since it had been several years since she had seen Susan. "It's so good to see you again, Marcia," Susan said as they embraced in a hug. "You can use the extra bed in my room. Angela's bedroom is much smaller."

After a few days of reliving college life and becoming familiar with her surroundings, Marcia was ready to survey the job market. Angela offered assistance by displaying her inventory of job openings and helping her prepare a resume.

Angela broke news about a new listing she had just received for a mathematics/computer science teacher at a private school. She shared the particulars with Marcia. "You'll be a good fit for this job; would you like me to submit your resume?"

"Yes, please do. It appears to be a job I would enjoy."

Darwin Academy was a small, elite, co-educational school for students from well-to-do families. The scholastic standards were high, and most of their graduates went on to attend four year colleges and universities. The faculty was a close knit group; most of them had been with the school for several years and enjoyed a genuine camaraderie. Its headmaster, Gordon Quenelle, was a stern, no nonsense disciplinarian who had earned the respect of both the faculty and the student body.

Two weeks after submitting her resume, Marcia and several other candidates were called in for interviews. The panel of interviewers scrutinized the qualifications and compared their notes on each candidate. Marcia's sold work record coupled with her *summa cum laude* honors tipped the scales in her favor. She was offered the position and accepted it.

Marcia brought with her a strong work ethic and sincere desire to educate her students. She fell right in with the faculty and had no difficulty pleasing her superior.

The school was located a short distance from one of the branch libraries which she often visited in connection with her work. Parking her 911 Carrera Turbo S coupe Porsche next to an identical Porsche gave her reason to ponder what the odds must be for that to happen; same model, same year, same color – maybe a million to one. As she started to leave, the owner of the other car approached. She inquired, "Is this some kind of Porsche festival?"

He smiled. "Looks like it could be. I was almost confused about which one to board until I saw you next to yours. I won't ask you how you enjoy driving it because I know the answer."

"It's a dream. But I refuse to become attached to it as I would a pet."

"Got to get back to the office. Nice talking to you."

Marcia thought he was a nice guy. *Handsome, too. I should have been more friendly.*

CHAPTER TWENTY-ONE

The teaching position was demanding. Marcia's social life was not suffering, but it did require some juggling. She and Jerry Hampton, an English teacher at Darwin, became friendly and enjoyed many evenings together.

At the end of each school day, students assembled in a designated area to await pickup by either a parent or another person designated on a computerized listing. Teachers were assigned to oversee the process, on a schedule that rotated weekly.

Marcia, on her assigned work week, had released about half the students when a request was made to pick up a student named Roger Clark. When she looked up, she recognized the man she had seen at the library.

"Well, if it isn't the Porsche Lady."

"And you are the Porsche Man. I need to see your I.D."

"Hmm. I see by your driver's license that you are Benson Jeffrey. Mr. Jeffrey, you're not on our authorization list for Roger Clark."

"I'm in law practice with Roger's dad. He's away on a business trip and asked me to handle this chore. Here's my business card."

"Mr. Jeffrey, we have strict rules here. If we allow these children to leave with an unauthorized person, we open ourselves up to all kinds of problems."

"As an attorney, I can certainly appreciate that."

"What about Mrs. Clark? She's on our list."

"Mrs. Clark is out of state, too."

"Well, I'm breaking the rules, but I don't have much choice. Your card does show that you are with the same firm as Mr. Clark, and I can't leave the child at school overnight. But please do me a favor. Take this authorization form and have Mr. Clark sign it as soon as he returns. Then get it back to me so I can place it in my file and log it into our computer, okay?"

"Sure. Thanks."

"I would never make a good attorney," Marcia said.

"Why?"

"An attorney would hold the kid overnight," she replied with a broad smile.

"You're funny. You know we're not that bad."

The next week Mr. Jeffrey returned the paper to Marcia.

"Just as I promised, here is your signed form. I owe you a favor."

"No need for that. I'm covered now, and I can breathe much easier."

"I was hoping to treat you to dinner. That actually would be a favor from you to me, though, instead of the other way around."

"Let me think about it."

"Your time is up."

"You seem determined. Okay. When and where?"

Ben smiled. "What about Saturday? I'll phone to get directions to your place and we can decide where to go later."

"Sounds good to me."

The couple ended up at the Ravenwood Country Club, where Ben was a member and a familiar figure to the staff and employees. Marcia was impressed by the surroundings and the attention they received from the wait staff. She thoroughly enjoyed the evening.

Ben explained to Marcia that he came from several generations of attorneys. He was now the only survivor, since his father had died from a heart attack when he was still in his fifties. His firm, Clark Jeffrey & Janowitz dealt with grand theft, embezzlements, corporate mergers, and takeovers. They often worked with bankers and CEOs.

Ben and Marcia hit it off and continued seeing each other. Both tall, they were a striking and imposing couple, displaying an air of confidence and importance. He had been accustomed to playing the field and enjoying the role of gadabout, but now he was ready to settle down. Their courtship was filled with the finest wine, food, and leisure. Marcia enjoyed every minute. Marriage was inevitable.

After the wedding, Marcia continued her work at the academy, knowing she was making a positive impression on her students. Her dedication often meant extra hours that sometimes extended into weekends.

Although they appeared to have been made for each other during the early years of their marriage, as time passed Ben began to lose interest. He wondered if he had made the right choice with Marcia.

Four years of Marcia's long hours of teaching and frequent absences from home, plus her not being sufficiently attentive to Ben, compounded the problem. She knew that many things were not in harmony, but was determined to make her marriage work.

PART FIVE

CHAPTER TWENTY-TWO

Jeff Benson's psychosomatic symptoms lingered on, and he struggled with his work assignments, especially those requiring intense mental concentration. Rex again advised him to take an extended leave, and again suggested a visit to Jeff's brother, David, in Seattle.

Earlier, Jeff had refused, not wanting his brother to see him in his present condition. This time, though, he reasoned that at some time David would learn the truth, so why not now?

"You know, you're right. I haven't seen my niece since she was three. I'm going."

"That's it, 'Uncle Jeff,' now you're talking!"

It was a joyous occasion when David, his wife Marilyn, and a grinning six year old Coletta greeted Jeff at the airport. David and Marilyn had agreed to accept Jeff for a two month stay. They provided him with a mother-in-law suite which allowed enough privacy for the entire family.

Jeff spent most of his time in leisure/sporting events and sailing. He even took a quick trip to Glacier Bay National Park in Alaska. But there was not so much self-indulgence that he could not find time and enjoyment reading to Colette.

"Colette is smart," Jeff told David. "And I want her to be smarter. That's why I'm reading to her. Stories at this age will encourage her to read and excel at school."

Jeff had ended his sessions with Dr. Zachery before his trip to Seattle, because the hypnosis no longer seemed to be helping. However, the doctor encouraged him to call if ever he felt his condition was worsening.

The visit proved to be good therapy. Jeff enjoyed his leisure and his reunion with his brother and his family. Most of his psychosomatic symptoms subsided.

Before the visit was over, however, Jeff ate some contaminated salmon and became very sick. He was nauseated, ran a high fever, and had trouble breathing.

Even though David was a physician, he first dismissed these symptoms as a return of Jeff's psychosomatic seizures. Later he correctly diagnosed the ailment as *e-coli* food poisoning, and admitted Jeff to the hospital where he worked. Treatments for the poisoning were effective; however, some of the psychological behaviors began to reappear, including imaginary knee pain. David decided to consult with Dr. Zachery.

After two weeks, Jeff was finally released from the hospital. Under his brother's constant observation and care he was soon almost back to normal.

When Rex, who was anxiously awaiting Jeff's return, heard about Jeff's troubles, he asked his wife, Becky, "What else can possibly happen to him?"

CHAPTER TWENTY-THREE

The divorce between Howard and Clara was quick and uncontested. Howard transferred to Culver Air Force Base in the Mojave Desert. Clara opted to relocate to Los Angeles. She cashed in all of her retirement funds and savings and vacation allowances to pay for the relocation. She found a moderately priced one bedroom apartment in Glendale and was able to pay cash for a Honda.

Clara's hunt for a job was now her number one priority. In the *Los Angeles Times*, she saw several positions listed by Prime Office Experts. Two of the postings caught her interest and she was eager to pursue both of them. She phoned the agency, faxed her resume to them, and managed to arrange a meeting for the next afternoon with one of their reps, Jennifer Baxter.

Clara knew how important appearances were in an interview. She dressed accordingly to project a professional image: light blue loose fitting blouse, dark skirt, half heeled shoes and a minimum of makeup and jewelry. Her resume was packed with extraordinary job duties and achievements, thanks to Major Stowe, her former supervisor.

The first interview that Jennifer arranged for Clara, with Culver Smith and Fugate, went well. The attorneys even talked salary-- $52,000 per year.

Clara's next interview, with the Clark Jeffrey Janowitz law firm, went even better. This position seemed considerably more appealing than the earlier one in every respect. The office was located in a nicer part of the city, and its office furnishings had the look of success.

Mr. Clark: "I see from your resume that Major Stowe delegated some important duties to you."

Clara: "Major Stowe was on flying status and was away from the office on TDY for several days at a time. Being the only person in the office, I was by default left in charge. I relished that responsibility."

Mr. Janowitz: "What were some of the duties you performed?"

Clara: "I drafted and typed wills, powers of attorney, personal property sales agreements, court martial charges, and a variety of other documents. Usually, Major Stowe gave my work only a cursory review and signed off on them."

Mr. Jeffrey: "Did you have a notary license?"

Clara: "Yes."

Mr. Jeffrey: "What kind of pressures or deadlines did you encounter?"

Clara: "I selected members of Court Martial while Major Stowe was away. This meant I had to approve and notify each member. Often these functions were time sensitive."

Mr. Jeffrey: "Did your boss ever question your judgment about the selections."

Clara: "No."

Mr. Clark: "Were you ever in a supervisory capacity?"

Clara: "When the workload became heavy, I enlisted the help of the central steno pool. I had to direct the work of three or four clerks."

Mr. Janowitz: "Would you anticipate any problem in performing our work as opposed to military legal work?"

Clara: "Not at all. There would be some differences, of course, but I'm adaptable and a person with high energy."

Mr. Jeffrey: "How do you feel about working extra hours?"

Clara: "I'll do whatever it takes to get the job done."

Mr. Clark: "How would you summarize this interview? Why should we offer you this position?"

Clara: "I'm ambitious. I want to excel in my job and make my supervisor look good, too. The end result will carry over to the success of this firm."

Mr. Jeffrey: "Thank you for coming."

Clara: "Thank you."

Clara left the building full of anticipation. She felt she had responded to each question with confidence, had remembered to smile frequently, and had exhibited friendliness and good nature.

Benson Jeffrey, as the spokesman for the group, had told Clara that they would give her a yes or no answer within three days.

After two days, Jennifer called Clara to say that the first firm had offered her the position she had interviewed for. Clara refused, saying the salary would be insufficient. *With that salary I would have to live like a wharf rat. I can't take that job.*

The third day passed with no word from Mr. Jeffrey. Clara called Jennifer to see what she might have learned.

"No word yet."

"Let me know the minute you hear."

"I will."

The fourth day passed.

The fifth day passed.

Damn. I'm really antsy. Why don't they respond? I'm beginning to worry. My funds are getting dangerously low!

On day six, Jennifer called to say the firm wanted a follow up interview.

Clara was puzzled. *What's going on?*

The next day Clara sat down with Benson Jeffrey in his office. He apologized for the delay, explaining that the partnership wanted to review a revised job description and that he had had a difficult time getting all the members together.

Mr. Jeffrey said, "Forget the job description we covered during your interview. The revised description is one you will like much better. It's a supervisory position with more responsibility and, of course, more pay. You would start at $92K a year. You would be on probation for the first sixty days, after which we could bump your salary to six figures. That is, after your references check out and everything is okay."

"That's great. I'm ready to begin."

"One other thing. It's not listed on the job description, but we're expanding and I want you to be a mentor to two rookies just out of law school."

"I can handle that."

Clara began her new job in earnest.

CHAPTER TWENTY FOUR

When the time came for Clara's two month probation to end, the partners all agreed to give her permanent status. She had proved to be a valuable asset, always willing to pitch in to see the job through.

The firm landed an important case involving a multi-million dollar merger. It had everyone in a buzz and eager to get to work.

Ben Jeffrey had the lead role. It was a delicate and high profile case requiring the utmost care.

"I want you to give this case your undivided attention, Clara. If you decide to delegate any of the assignments, I want close supervision from you."

"I understand. There will be no slip ups."

The merger went through better than expected. The regulatory bodies found no evidence of monopolistic advantages and gave their approval. For a victory celebration, Ben gave a party at the Ravenwood for all staff members. The mood was cheerful, if not exhilarating, and continued until several decided to depart.

*****

Joe Westbrook's firm, Alliance and Associates, was offering returns of 15-20 percent, and the word soon spread to others who wanted to share in this lucrative payout. As long as new investors were feeding the kitty – a classic Ponzi scheme – this practice continued unabated. When new funding dried up, however, the bottom fell out.

Some time later Alliance ceased operations, leaving investors without their promised returns; without even the original principal itself. Gilbert Devron lost most of the $450,000 he had hoped would give him security in his retirement. Despondent and embittered over his loss, he wanted retribution without mercy. His networking with others who had also lost money led them to the Clark Jeffrey Janowitz law firm.

Clara, eager to impress her superiors, had found out from courthouse records searches that Joe Westbrook had gone through a hotly contested divorce a few years earlier. His ex, a woman named Shirley Bates Westbrook, was now living in Scottsdale, Arizona. During a phone call to her, Clara was not at all surprised to hear about Shirley's unpleasant memories. None of the revelations seemed to be useful, until Shirley mentioned that Joe had a twenty five year old son from an earlier marriage who was living in Venezuela. That knowledge was to prove crucial during and after the trial.

The case ended as a class action suit involving 87 litigants. Joe Westbrook was found guilty on all counts of fraud, money laundering and misrepresenting the appropriateness of the investments. The presiding judge handed him a ten year prison sentence and ordered him to liquidate his assets, including cars, boats, and a private airplane.

To celebrate this victory, the partnership once again gave a party at their usual venue, the Ravenwood.

Ben took Clara to an adjoining conference room to extend special congratulations.

"You played a key role in this case. If you had not found out about Joe's son living in Venezuela, I am certain Joe would have jumped bail and would be living there now. The US does not have an extradition agreement with that country, and that is why the judge made him surrender his passport. Clara, I want you to know how much I appreciate your contribution to the success of this endeavor. I like to see that kind of initiative."

"Thank you. We all worked hard. I suppose I got lucky." Clara smiled, knowing that had made points with her boss.

"How did you acquire your good work habits?"

"I grew up in West Texas – an only child. My dad was an accountant and my mother was a school teacher. I was taught that hard work is rewarding in every way." Clara was becoming comfortable in lying about her background.

"I could tell from the very beginning that you had a quality upbringing. I've always prided myself on being a good judge of character. I know yours is exemplary. I'm really pleased you're part of the team. I just wish we had more people around with your character traits."

"Mr. Jeffrey, you're making me feel too good about myself."

"I'll go one step further. You know how to dress and how to act to project a good image for our firm. Some would even say your looks are pleasing."

"You're making me blush."

Clara left that evening with the idea she was on track. *I've got to be patient, and keep on being coy.*

CHAPTER TWENTY-FIVE

Marcia Jeffrey wanted to be with her husband more often, but her teaching kept demanding more and more of her time. When she was told she had to attend a mandatory week long retreat – away from school – she seriously considering quitting. But her dedication to Gordon Quenelle and the Academy just would not allow that. The work was interfering with her married life, and she knew she must come to grips with this dilemma.

With Marcia away at her retreat, Ben asked Clara to join him for pizza after work. Of course she agreed. He asked, "Would you call Antonio's and place an order for our pizzas and beer? Make mine pepperoni and sausage and Heineken."

That evening business talk soon ceased and small talk took over.

"Are you dating anyone now, Clara?"

"Yes, you were gone when Paul came by the office and we lunched together."

"I would like to have met him. What does he do?"

"He's in sales – wholesale sporting goods."

"Have you known him long?"

"Only a couple of months. We're not serious."

Ben moved closer. "Don't get too serious with anyone. I don't want to lose you."

"Don't worry, I'm staying. I enjoy my job and all the people I work with."

"Including me?"

"Yes, especially you, Mr. Jeffrey. You've been very generous with me."

"You can call me Ben after office hours,"

"The pizza and beer really hit the spot. Thank you ... Ben."

"My pleasure. Perhaps we can repeat a relaxing evening together again soon. What if we have dinner at my place tomorrow evening?"

"I don't think that would be a good idea, with Marcia gone on her school retreat."

Ben let the matter drop, and soon they parted amicably.

"Good night ... Ben."

"Good night, Clara."

The next day at work was uneventful until late in the afternoon. Ben came by Clara's office to say, "You don't really want me to have dinner alone, do you?"

"Mr. Jeffrey, you undoubtedly have friends or golfing buddies who could join you."

"Sure I do, but I would enjoy your company much more. I know a good Chinese place. Do you like Chinese food?"

"Oh, yes"

"Then will you join me?"

"I'm not sure."

"I'll be by your place at seven."

"Well ... okay."

The Golden Dragon was a fine dining restaurant with all the trappings of real class. Attention to details and service to patrons was of the highest order. Ben saw to it that all of Clara's needs were met. As they were leaving the premises, Clara thanked Ben for an enjoyable evening.

The drive back took an unfamiliar route. Clara was quick to mention to Ben that he was not on the way to her apartment.

"Chinese food is not very filling. I thought perhaps we could stop by my house for a dessert and coffee."

"You don't recall the concern I mentioned yesterday?"

"Don't concern yourself."

"Looks like I'm a captive."

When they arrived at his home, Ben took two strawberry tarts from the freezer, popping them into the microwave. Decaffeinated coffee was soon steaming in two mugs. Ben put his arm around Clara's waist, declaring, "This is what it's all about."

"Don't you want to eat your dessert?"

"No, I have a better dessert in my arms."

"Ben, don't forget; you're a married man. Marcia will be hurt."

The kisses and caresses kept coming. Clara's weak resistance was no match for Ben's aggressive determination. She was overcome with such emotional affection, she forgot how the play acting was supposed to go. Ben was pleasantly surprised to find how eager Clara was to receive his lovemaking.

The wee hours of the morning had crept up on them when Ben suggested she spend the remainder of the night there.

"I'll drive you home in an hour or two so you'll have time to freshen up before work."

"Fine. I'll certainly need to do that." Clara knew now that the hook had been set.

CHAPTER TWENTY-SIX

Marcia Jeffrey, returning from her retreat, felt she could no longer postpone her decision. She asked for and was granted a leave of absence from the Academy. A replacement was not easy to find, but after a lot of digging, an available substitute was found. Now Marcia and Ben could enjoy evenings together at home. Also, now she could occasionally pitch in at her husband's law office, helping out wherever she could be useful.

Marcia and Clara became good friends. They often performed assignments together. Marcia marveled at Clara's energy and enthusiasm to get the jobs done. Often they would get together on their lunch period to eat, talk girl talk, and sip martinis.

It was this closeness that enabled Marcia to confide some of her personal feelings to Clara. During one of their lunches Marcia said, "Clara, I sense that Ben is losing interest in me and my relations with him."

"What exactly has happened?"

"I can't pinpoint the specifics, but I've seen that he's become distant, withdrawn, and indifferent to my needs and feelings."

"Maybe he's working too hard. Or, maybe the two of you need to get away for a few days."

"I hope it doesn't get worse. I've worked hard to make our marriage a success."

"You two make a good couple."

"Thanks. We'd better get back to the office before we both get fired."

Ben soon found a way to bring Clara to him again. "Clara, I hope you don't have important things to do over this weekend."

"Nothing that I can't forego. Do you have a weekend job for me?"

"Yes. Can you come in on Saturday?"

"I think so. What time?"

"Let's say ten."

"I'll be here. What does this job involve?"

"Mostly catch-up stuff. I'm behind on an embezzlement case."

Clara wasn't so dumb; she knew Ben wanted a repeat encounter. She rehearsed in her mind just how she would react to his advances.

On Saturday the two met as planned. Ben did not immediately engage in personal talk, lest Clara would suspect his real motive.

After about two hours of mundane sorting and filing, Ben suggested a lunch break. They went to Plato's, a nearby cafe that specialized in Greek food – mostly gyros. After placing their orders, Ben initiated the conversation. "Clara, if you haven't suspected already, Marcia and I have a marriage that is breaking apart."

"Marcia has told me about your problems."

"I've lost all interest in her and in keeping our marriage intact."

"That's too bad. Are you telling me it can't be salvaged?"

"Yes. It would be futile to try. Marcia has tried to make a go of it."

"I'm sorry."

"The reason I'm telling you – I don't want you to feel guilty over what we've done. The marriage was on the rocks before you came along."

"Maybe I should feel less guilty, but I've never been intimate with a married guy before," she lied.

"For all practical purposes, I'm not married ... just legally."

"Let's get back to the office."

Ben's amorous moves began soon after they returned. They kissed and he led Clara over to the couch. "Ben, I do care for you, but I would feel better if we waited until after your divorce."

"I can't wait."

CHAPTER TWENTY-SEVEN

During the next several weeks the romance between Ben and Clara continued. Ben found an out of the way motel where he could rent a room by just walking in. No questions asked.

Clara's anxiousness was beginning to make her feel that she was being used. She consulted the firm's log of staff birthdays, anniversaries, etc. and found that Ben and Marcia were approaching their fifth wedding anniversary. The wheels in her conniving mind began to turn. *I've got to bring this relationship to a head, and I know just how to do it.*

The next afternoon the two women lunched together, and Clara innocently asked Marcia if she was still encountering difficulties in her marriage.

"Yes. It is actually becoming worse."

Clara then offered this advice: "Sometimes a trip can be refreshing. I noticed in our log book that your anniversary is only three weeks away. What if I arranged for the two of you to retrace your honeymoon trip?"

"Clara, you're a genius!"

The day before the anniversary, Clara arranged an after work party at Ravenwood. She spared no expense for the celebration – wine, champagne, music, and even an emcee. The revelry continued for several hours. Then Clara gave Ben and Marcia copies of their itinerary complete with reservations and travel tickets.

CHAPTER TWENTY-EIGHT

Back in San Diego, while reviewing their work assignments, Jeff Benson and Rex Newton noted that a final review of their newest shopping center in Las Vegas was scheduled for the next Tuesday. All major elements of the project were already in place; just the formality of a meeting with the committee and the state fire marshal remained.

Rex asked, "Are you up to the task, Jeff?"

"Oh, yeah. If I lapse into a trance, I'll just excuse myself and leave the room."

Rex added, "Greg and Tim delivered the model yesterday. They did a terrific job. We need to remember that when their annual performance reviews come up."

Jeff arrived at McCarran Airport at four and checked into the Arabian Nights Hotel at six o'clock. After a steak and lobster dinner he studied the prints one last time, then hit the hay.

CHAPTER TWENTY-NINE

Ben and Marcia Jeffrey left John Wayne Airport on Tuesday at two o'clock, arriving in Las Vegas in time for a few hours of leisure before dinner. They attended a show on the strip and returned to the Arabian Nights Hotel about ten o'clock.

After settling into their suite, an amorous Marcia approached Ben with a come-on look. She wanted this escape and could not remember when she had been so horny. Ben only smiled, then walked away to brush his teeth and undress for bed. Aloof and oblivious to Marcia's overtures, he yawned and pulled the covers back. Marcia undressed and planted her nude body next to Ben. At that moment Ben rolled over, with his back to her. In a few minutes she heard a snore. Aghast, she moved away, and sat up on the edge of the bed.

Am I that obnoxious? She stared at the diamond design on the carpet. *Is this any way to celebrate an anniversary? What's wrong with him? Can I continue to tolerate this kind of neglect?* She rubbed her hand across her forehead. *I refuse to feel sorry for myself, dejected as I am. Right now I can't possibly sleep. I've got to get out of here.*

Marcia dressed and as she left the room, the click of the door latch sounded all too loud and certain. *Dammit! I've locked myself out.* She remembered seeing the plastic key card on the dresser and had intended to take it, but with her mental acuities hampered, she had just plain forgotten. Her fist was drawn back to knock on the door, but she stopped short. *Ben is sound asleep. No need to wake him yet. I'll get a duplicate key downstairs.*

The hotel lobby was still crowded and noisy. *A drink might calm me, but first I'll go outside and get some fresh air.*

To help clear her mind, Marcia sat on a bench facing the broad sidewalk. At that late hour, there was still steady foot traffic. A game of people guessing popped into her mind. She and Ben had played it before. The first person she spotted walking down the sidewalk was a large, moon faced dude wearing a Stetson. He had an open collar adorned with a gold necklace. His swagger had that million dollar look. Marcia's take: *He's a used car salesman.*

Next she saw a couple of elderly ladies walking side by side. They both had that stern, serious aspect familiar from school days. *They've got to be retired teachers.*

The steady parade of people was not so unusual until a couple came strolling by hand in hand. The gent appeared to be in his mid-fifties. Rotund in the middle with narrow shoulders, he surely was not someone given to physical exertion. His white wavy hair flowing behind his ears made him even more noticeable. Alligator shoes and pearl cuff links suggested wealth.

His escort, a bottle blonde perhaps in her mid-twenties, was clinging tightly to his folded elbow. She kept looking up adoringly to his smiling face. Equally adorned in high fashion, she sported a green and white designer suit matched with a necklace of several diamonds set in a cluster of emeralds.

Marcia's guess – no, this was not a guess, she was sure it was a slam dunk – *he's a televangelist and has known his girlfriend for less than 24 hours!*

Marcia sighed. *This game is not as much fun when only one person plays. You need someone else to provide feedback. Time for a drink.* She walked back into the lobby and over to a small bar in the corner.

"What'll it be?" shouted the bartender, who was decked out in a red vest and black bow tie. She was wearing a large plastic name tag with "Peggy" in large letters. She smiled often and talked in a loud voice to get the attention of all patrons.

Peggy was one of those persons who would be a challenge for a hairdresser or makeup artist. She really was not ugly, but her long flowing red hair did not seem to belong with a ruddy complexion. Her western twang was not an improvement. She strutted around with the confidence and self esteem worthy of a Nobel Prize laureate.

"I'll have a martini. Make sure to use Bombay Sapphire gin."

"Coming right up. Lady, excuse me for saying this, but you look awful."

"Do I really look that bad?"

"Maybe you want to talk about it?"

"Not unless you can give me a pep talk."

"That's my specialty! So, what happened?"

Marcia turned the conversation back to the bartender. "Are you married?"

"Yes."

"Are you happily married?"

"I suppose so."

"What's the secret to your success?"

"No secret. And actually this is my second time around."

"So what happened in your first marriage?"

"Jack and me – we both had roving eyes. After two years of jealous spats we called it quits. Our marriage wasn't all bad. We have the cutest, most adorable little guy you could ever imagine. Jack has custody, but I have visitation rights."

"What about your present husband, Peggy?"

"Reggie is a good guy. Works hard. He's a decent person."

"What does he do?"

"He's a maintenance man – works out at Nellis."

"So, you're saying that your second time around is better?"

"Oh, yeah. Much better. I would say happy marriages happen some times, just because of the odds. You know, like gambling here in Vegas."

Marcia finished her martini and stood up. "It's been nice talking with you. You've been helpful."

Marcia walked over to the front desk, sheepishly telling the attendant that she had locked herself out.

"Happens all the time, ma'am. What's the room number?"

"I don't know. My husband checked us in. All I know is that it is on the third floor."

"What's the name?"

"Benson Jeffrey."

"I need to see your driver's license."

The clerk input the name into the computer. "Here it is. That's room 346." He handed her a plastic key card enclosed in the familiar small brown paper envelope.

Marcia took the elevator to the third floor, walked down the hall, and inserted the key into the slot. Without making a noise, she quietly made her way to the area between the bathroom and an adjacent area lit only by a weak night light. A light in the bathroom would be too bright, she reasoned, so she decided to undress right there.

It was Jeff, not Ben, who by now had roused and was half awake. Marcia, unaware, slipped off all her clothing, then moved toward the bed and placed her wristwatch on the night stand. Next, she removed each of her earrings and placed them next to the watch.

When Jeff, still groggy, looked up he saw a beautiful woman with backlighting giving her face a gently glowing aura. He was unable to comprehend the situation. Time seemed to stop. The woman's majestic image gave him a flashback to his wedding night. *What's happening? Is Rex behind this?*

When Marcia came over to lie in bed, Jeff rolled over to move closer to her. Inhibitions resulting from his trauma were completely gone. He put his strong arms around her, like the strong arms she knew so well.

Marcia was surprised. *Is Ben having second thoughts about his earlier spurn?* A kiss on the neck. Then more kisses on the neck. When their lips touched, she detected some difference, but her love starved feelings were by now so intense that she was not truly aware that this was not Ben. She became so absorbed in her strange lover that she was entirely oblivious to her surroundings.

Jeff's memory of the halo was gone. The exhilarating moment at hand was so powerful that any past thoughts were erased from his mind.

The climactic ending was perfect for both Jeff and Marcia. A contrast of stillness settled for a while. Marcia arose and announced, "What a great evening. I hope you enjoyed it as much as I did."

"Yes, it was wonderful."

Marcia stood still. "Your voice, Ben – are you coming down with a cold?" She flicked the light switch.

"E-e-e-e-yow! You are not Ben! What are you doing in my ro--?!"

"Lady, I'm sorry. This is not your room."

She realized what had happened and made a mad rush to the bathroom, grabbing her clothes as she went. She returned fully dressed, shouting, "You bastard! You've ruined my life, my marriage." As she was about to slam the door, Marcia left Jeff with these parting words: "Don't gloat over this very long. You haven't heard the last of it. There's more to come."

Jeff responded in a quiet voice, "I'm sorry."

Marcia left in a fit of anger and humiliation. *Just wait till I confront that idiot at the front desk.* On her way to the lobby, she looked into the elevator mirror to see a disheveled, half dressed person who was in no condition to confront anyone.

There was a ladies room just off the lobby downstairs, and she ducked in to neaten herself. When she opened her purse to its cosmetics compartment, she saw it. What a revelation! The room key ... the original one. *Ben must've put it there while I was dealing with the porter.*

The crew at the front desk had changed shifts. There was no reason to confront them now since they would not know what I was talking about. *Besides, now I've calmed down. This sudden turn of events is too much for me to understand. I need to think. Should I tell Ben? What should I say if I do?* Marcia sat on a couch in the lobby until she felt herself begin to relax. I won't do anything – if at all – until tomorrow. A cool head should prevail.

The next morning Ben said, "Clara phoned while you were in the shower. The staff was able to locate the key witness in the McAlister case. They're sure he's now in Reno. I've got to go and talk to him."

"Oh, no! Why you?" Marcia responded. "Can't someone else go?"

"No, I'm the only one familiar with the details."

"Couldn't someone else take a deposition?"

"I don't want to take that chance. He might leave the country. He's a citizen of Austria here on a temporary visa."

"Damn! Our anniversary is falling to pieces."

"It shouldn't take more than two days. We can meet in Flagstaff, go to the Grand Canyon, and then Tahiti."

"I'm not happy, but maybe I can live with it."

At eight o'clock Ben and Marcia were sitting in the hotel cafe, ordering breakfast, when the hostess seated Jeff at the only available spot – two tables away, facing Marcia.

"Ben, would you mind trading chairs with me?"

"No, not at all. But why? Are you uncomfortable?"

"No, it's just that the scenery I'm facing is not to my liking."

Ben shrugged and they swapped places.

After breakfast a waiter approached Ben with the information that his taxi was waiting. Ben rose and kissed Marcia on the cheek. "I've just got time to catch that 10:30 flight to Reno. Bye, now. See you in a couple of days."

Ben left with his briefcase and a small overnight bag.

Jeff looked at Ben, then looked again. *What am I seeing? Is he my twin? My clone? Same everything – height, body build, even his stride. This is not real.*

He waited until he saw Marcia leave the dining area, then followed her to the main lobby. "Lady," he called. "Can we talk?"

"Only if you have something of substance to say; like, who are you?"

Jeff gave her his business card and gestured for her to sit in one of two upholstered chairs. He seated himself in the other one.

Reading his card, Marcia said, "So you're Jeffrey Benson?" The name immediately struck a chord she kept to herself. "Are you married?"

"I'm a widower. May I have your name?"

"Marcia Jeffrey."

"I'm truly sorry for what happened, and I want to offer you any help I can."

"My biggest concern at the moment is whether I might have caught something."

"Please be assured that your catching anything from me is impossible. I haven't been intimate with a woman for over a year."

"Whoa! What are you telling me? You are single. You have just banged me, and I'm supposed to believe that you are all pure and innocent?"

"I know it's hard to believe, but it's the truth. I've had a psychosomatic illness since I lost my wife. All these months my life has been miserable. I've been under the care of a psychiatrist."

"Then how do you explain what happened between us?"

"I know this will sound weird, but when I saw you undressing in my room, I saw the same image of my wife on our wedding night. I had a flashback."

Marcia, still angry and provoked, allowed herself to make an uncharacteristically catty remark. "Have you heard of Rod Serling? You could be one up on him easily. Actually, your story is so bizarre, I don't think you could have made it up."

"If you want proof, I can furnish names of my medications, my psychiatrist, my business partner, my wife's death certificate – any kind of proof you ask for."

"You seem to be okay now."

Jeff said, "You know, I feel cured. It's like some spirit has swooped down with a magic wand. I no longer sense any of the symptoms. My concern is that you don't experience any kind of trauma after this. Certainly nothing like mine."

"I still think you're a skunk."

Then she departed.

CHAPTER THIRTY

Jeff wanted Marcia to know he was sincere about his apology. Before going to his ten o'clock appointment with the review committee, he went around to the other side of the lobby to the desk of the hotel concierge to place an order.

"I want a dozen long stemmed red roses, complete with vase, delivered to Mrs. Marcia Jeffrey. Be sure the gratuity is prepaid. Charge it to my room. Here's my key card."

"Any message?"

"I'm ready to help."

The meeting with the building committee was uneventful. It was more of a formality than one with a tough give and take. The state fire marshal asked a few easily answered questions, and that was it.

Back in his room, Jeff phoned the office to give a status report. "Rex, the shopping center is a done deal. The meeting was a breeze. I want you to know I have had no hint of any health problems. I feel great. No depression, no staring, no memory lapses. I'm cured."

"I'm so glad to hear that. I can't wait till you get back and start being your old self again."

"Me, too. See you."

Jeff plopped onto the bed. Staring up at the ceiling he was happy to feel such a certainty that his trauma was cured. Then his thoughts turned to the time when he had witnessed the bereavement of Mai Lois in Costa Rica. He wondered if it was over now; maybe through the passage of time, or maybe through some special event. Surely she would have experience nothing like what had happened to him. At any rate, he reassured himself that she must have met "Mr. Right" by now.

Shortly after noon the roses were delivered to Marcia's room. She was surprised, of course, thinking they had been sent by Ben. When she saw Jeff's name on the card, she immediately dropped the flowers into the waste basket ... vase and all.

Nothing worked to relieve her mind of thinking about the night before. She had not heard anything from Ben, which made matters worse. First she tried a crossword puzzle, but could not concentrate. The TV was not the answer, either. She flung herself across the bed and began to cry. The crying continued on and on. After an hour or so, she finally arose, grabbed the complimentary $200 worth of casino tokens the hotel had provided with the room, and went downstairs.

The poker slots were very active. Marcia noticed that the player next to her had exhausted his tokens without a win, and surmised that now the same machine might be lucky for her. No such luck, however, and she was down to her last token when Jeff appeared.

"I thought I might find you here. I wanted to look you up so I could return your watch and earrings. Here."

"Thanks."

"Have you won anything yet, Marcia?"

"No. I've never been a good gambler."

"Neither have I."

Marcia started to rise.

"Don't leave. I've not yet used any of my complimentary tokens. Let's continue to feed this monster."

Jeff sat down, and had used about half of his tokens when the 7-8-9 and 10 of hearts plus the six of spades appeared on the screen.

"Shall we cash out? This straight would pay four to one."

Marcia was noncommittal.

Jeff held the four hearts and asked for a draw card. Incredibly, the six of hearts appeared.

Marcia screamed with joy and lunged at Jeff, locking her arms around his neck. Then she stopped. *I didn't mean to do that. I got carried away.* She quickly let go.

The machine cranked out so many tokens they needed an extra bucket to hold them. When the cashier counted out the win, it totaled over two grand.

Marcia said, "You really hit the jackpot."

Jeff responded, "No, not me. The jackpot is yours."

"I'll split it with you," Marcia offered.

"I've got a better idea. I'll let you buy me a drink."

They entered the bar area and took a booth in the corner. Jeff asked, "What had you planned to do this evening?"

Marcia replied, "I've not made any plans. Maybe watch TV."

"Would you be opposed to having dinner with me?"

"Yes, I would be opposed. We've seen enough of each other."

"Please? I can reserve a table at Wynn's. We can make amends. I'm not such a bad guy. Wouldn't that be better than watching TV?"

"Well, maybe you're right. Just food and talk, okay?"

"You're on."

Marcia stopped by the front desk. "Any messages for room 336?"

"No messages for you, ma'am."

She then went to her room and checked her iPhone. Nothing there. *Ben should have called by now.* She retrieved the vase of roses from the trash and placed it on the table. *Maybe I've been too hard on Jeff. After all, I was the one who went to his bed.*

At seven Jeff and Marcia met in the lobby and walked outside to hail a cab. While motoring to Wynn's, they both seemed to become more relaxed and amicable.

"I've been toying with some numbers," Marcia said. "We've challenged Guinness. What do you think the odds are for dealing a straight flush? One in 64,974! The chances are much better if you are dealt four cards in sequence of the same suit. It's now pretty good, 2 in 47. It seems there are spirits influencing my life!"

"You don't mean evil spirits?"

"No. Let's just say my inner feelings are strange."

"You've been through some unusual events."

At Wynn's the atmosphere was pleasant. It provided a quiet and peaceful time for them, contrasting with the hectic days they both had been through.

Marcia wanted to know, "What kind of marriage did you have, Jeff? It must have been good; else you would not have become mentally sick."

"It was great. Barbara was wonderful. Our love was agape love. Unremitting love. Love given that asks nothing in return. It was the same agape love that God has for his people."

"So unusual in this day and time."

"Yes," Jeff agreed.

"Jeff, there's a special favor I want to ask you."

"Anything. What is it?"

"I want you to drive me to Flagstaff tomorrow. I'm in no condition to drive. I don't trust myself."

"What's in Flagstaff?"

"Our dual wedding took place there. The first was a week earlier in LA. Ben and I will be reenacting the ceremony. I will be meeting him there."

"What happens when he sees me?"

"Don't worry. I'll come up with something."

The next morning Jeff and Marcia walked four blocks down the strip and two blocks down a side street to the pre-arranged car rental. After taking care of the paperwork, they were on their way. Soon concrete, steel, lights, and neon signs gave way to rocks and sand. Twenty minutes down Route 93 Marcia broke the silence. "You know, it's a crazy world out there."

"I agree," answered Jeff, "but what exactly do you mean?"

"Look over to your left. What do you see?" she rhetorically asked. "Shacks, Quonset huts, RV's and lean-tos. People are living there in squalor and we're only 20 miles from where other people think nothing of gambling high stakes of thousands of dollars. You would think we live in a third world country."

"I know. It's crazy and it's sad."

"Crazy yes!" she continued. "Two days ago I could have boiled you in oil. Now I'm befriending you and in your close company."

"I'm glad you've had a change in attitude."

They continued driving down Route 93 to Hoover Dam and Lake Mead.

Jeff said, "As an engineer, I'm truly amazed at this giant. Some day I might allow time to take an in-depth tour of it, but for now we need to keep going."

They stopped for lunch at Kingman, Arizona, then took Interstate 40 to travel eastward. A plaque on the side of the road named a site after Andy Devine. Marcia asked, "Who was he?"

"I recall he was a character actor in B westerns," Jeff replied.

The desert began to show some vegetation as they gained altitude. Marcia turned the radio on hoping to get some music and maybe a weather report. They were too far away from any stations to pick up any clear reception. Farther down the road the rental Mitsubishi began misfiring. Jeff surmised that the reason might be the altitude change. Later the problem seemed to correct itself.

The countryside became verdant, lush meadows and ponderosa forests. The air had a feeling of freshness.

Two hours later Marcia and Jeff crossed Route 66, made famous in song and television, then they reached the Sundown Inn Bed and Breakfast. A prominent shingle dangled over the front porch: "Est. 1902. Ten years before statehood."

They climbed the porch steps and were greeted by an elderly gentleman. "Yes sir and madam, what can I do for you?"

Marcia spoke up. We have a reservation. Mr. and Mrs. Jeffrey." She signed the register he proffered.

"Mrs. Jeffrey, you've been assigned a non-smoking room with a king bed. Number six."

"Can you change us to a room with two single beds instead of the king?" she asked.

"I'm not sure." The man peered up from his glasses, evidently suspicious, and stared – first at Jeff, then at Marcia.

Marcia quickly explained, "My husband snores."

"All our rooms are booked," he said. "Maybe I could move a cot in there. Would that do?"

Jeff spoke up, "Yeah, that'll be fine."

Their room was furnished with a bed, a desk, table, two chairs and a phone. Leafing through the inn's brochure that he found on the desk, Jeff learned that the place had once been a saloon, a sheriff's office, and a bordello; and had been an inn for the last thirty-two years.

Marcia was not impressed. Her mind was focused on other matters. She opened her purse and grabbed her iPhone.

"Who are you calling?" asked Jeff.

"Ron Jamison. He was the best man at our wedding."

Moments later Marcia slowly put her iPhone down.

"I don't like the look on your face. What's wrong?"

"Ron Jamison is out of town."

Marcia next called the law office. "Have you heard any word from Ben?"

Annette responded, "No word at all. Isn't he with you?"

"What about Clara?"

"She left two days ago. Didn't say where she was going; only that she wouldn't be back until Monday."

Marcia screamed, "What the hell is going on, there?" She clicked off the phone.

"Jeff, do you think I am naive?"

"No, not at all. Why do you ask?"

"Please place a call to the Cal-Nev Ponderosa Resort at Tahoe," she asked. "Here's what I want you to say." She then gave him the wording.

Jeff went to Google to get the resort's number, then placed the call. When he reached the resort, he asked to be connected to the room of Mr. and Mrs. Ben Jeffery.

A female voice answered.

"Hello! Mrs. Jeffrey?"

"Yes?"

"This is the resort management. I just wanted to make sure you found everything to your satisfaction."

"Yes, thank you. We're fine."

"Great. Have a good day."

Jeff broke the connection, then turned to Marcia. "You are a super sleuth. How did you know where to call?"

"It wasn't so difficult after I gave it some thought. That resort is where Ben and I stayed over long holiday weekends. Now that hussy is shacking up there with my husband. And to think I considered her a friend. Yes, I am naive."

"Maybe you just put too much trust in Ben. Sometimes there's a fine line between naiveté and being a trusting person.

"I should have suspected hanky-panky sooner. I remember when I returned home from a school retreat, I questioned Ben about the aroma of perfume in our bedroom. It was the unmistakable aroma of Clara's *L'Air du temps.* He shrugged it off, saying that he had worked in close contact with her at the office that day. This is definitely the end of our marriage."

"You won't try to salvage it in any way?"

"Not a chance."

"I'm sorry for you. You seem adamant about calling it quits. Aren't you devastated?"

"I would have been earlier. Knowing what I know now changes the whole picture. Devastated? No. Angry? Hell yes!"

"Does that mean that we can become more than just friends?" Jeff asked.

"No, not yet. I still want to honor my wedding vows until the ink dries on my divorce decree."

Removing a pearl earring from her lobe Marcia made a proclamation: "I'm dropping this earring on the floor. It will be just like that ball dropping on Times Square in New York City to start a new year. When you see this pearl hit the floor, that will be a sign that my life is taking an abrupt turn."

(Plop.)

"You can certainly be dramatic," Jeff opined. "I think you would be good at acting, or perhaps writing for a living."

"Enough of this. Jeff, are you game to celebrate?"

"You really are sincere about making a change, aren't you?"

"Yes, and I am ready to celebrate. What should we do?" She continued, "Maybe I should surprise you. Let's get in that poor excuse for a car. I'll direct you to a place I know you'll like."

Marcia checked to make sure the inn she had in mind was still in operation. She and Ben had gone there earlier during their honeymoon.

The Black Bear was an elongated nondescript building with a dining area large enough to seat 100 patrons. Up front, adjacent to the kitchen, was a bandstand. An old piano, still off key, sat squarely on it.

Jeff and Marcia found an empty table without the need for a hostess. Service was quick and the food was good. Rib-eye steaks and Coors beer. Four barbershop singers began a serenade: "Mazy, Mazy, give me your answer true ..."

Jeff and Marcia were absorbed in the entertainment. Soon it was time for sing-alongs, mostly songs from the Tin Pan Alley era. After three beers, it didn't matter if their singing was not in sync with the melody. They were both content to just be part of the happy crowd.

By the time they left the Black Bear, Marcia's speech was beginning to slur and her steps were a bit tottering. Jeff helped her into the car. He did not show the same effects; however, he wanted to make it back to the B'n'B without any mishaps.

After parking the Mitsubishi, Jeff directed Marcia to their room. He helped her undress, tucked her in the bed, and stepped over to the cot.

Marcia awoke the next morning feeling much better, and with no hint of a hangover. "Jeff," she said, "last night I was vulnerable, and you could have taken advantage of me. You didn't, and now my trust in you is unequivocal. You're very noble."

Jeff mused, *where have I heard that before? Mai Lois thought so, too.*

Breakfast was as good as they expected – they selected the works. The B'n'B prepared a box lunch for them, and Jeff and Marcia checked out and continued their journey, heading up scenic Route 180. Onward they drove, through miles and miles of aspens. It was late September, and at the higher altitudes the colors were at their peak. Some trees shone a bright primrose yellow, while others were of a more golden hue. Their leaves flashed alternating light and a range of subdued colors with each gust of wind. A few maverick leaves fell prematurely.

The couple stopped at a clearing off to the right and found a large log which had perhaps been swept down by a windstorm. There they spread their lunch.

If allowed, one could sense a feeling of eeriness, being surrounded by such a monolithic vastness. But a deep breath would negate that feeling with a rapture more than one would ever want to ask for. Each aspen must be in a state of euphoria, satisfying yet two more creatures much like others as their tree ancestors had been doing for millennia.

Marcia sat very still, then cocked her head slightly.

"Listen, Jeff, the trees are talking to us."

"I don't hear anything. Tell me what they are saying."

"They are telling us we can be happy just by being in their presence. Don't you feel that serenity and contentment when the air is still?"

"Well, yes, I do feel that I can really relax."

Marcia closed her eyes, took a deep breath, raised her arms over her head, and proclaimed: "I feel so wonderful, so carefree, so uninhibited."

Jeff mused, "How can we thank the aspens?"

CHAPTER THIRTY-ONE

The Grand Canyon appeared suddenly, as if it were a big surprise. The approach had given no clue as to what was to follow. Then, all at once, Jeff and Marcia were in the midst of colored splendor created over millions of years.

They finally found a place to park which offered an unobstructed view. The purple hues were especially brilliant against a clear blue sky. Far, far down below, hikers and mules were barely visible.

Marcia asked, "Is this your first trip here?"

"To the South Rim, yes. I've camped on the North Rim a few times as a Boy Scout. I can say the South Rim is much more spectacular. This sight is so ... so ... well, I'm lost for words."

They drove the length of the canyon to make sure they did not miss any vistas.

"I can never find my iPhone when I need it. A photo would be perfect right now." Marcia rummaged in her purse. "I must've left it behind."

Mine needs a charge. I guess we'll miss the enjoyment of looking at pictures in the weeks ahead."

"Well, we'd better go anyway. I have no idea what the check in time is at the hotel."

The El Tovar Hotel was a short distance away, still at the canyon site. Their reservations were intact. Marcia and Jeff needed only a minimum of time to settle in. This time the room had two single beds.

Jeff picked up the hotel's brochure and exclaimed, "How 'bout this guest list ... Albert Einstein, Elizabeth Taylor, and Paul McCartney."

"I'm impressed," Marcia said; then laughed and pointed to a small sign on the wall, which read: SOMNAMBULATING NOT ALLOWED. "Does that apply to you, Jeff?"

"What does it mean?"

"Sleepwalking. Just somebody's dumb joke." She added, "But really, only 30 yards from here the last step is treacherous ... straight off the South Rim."

"You can bet your sweet ass I won't leave my bed," Jeff answered solemnly.

CHAPTER THIRTY-TWO

Meanwhile, at the Cal-Nev Ponderosa Resort, Ben and Clara were together for their third day.

"It's great to get away from the office," Ben said.

"This is a fabulous place, Ben. It has everything. The horseback ride this morning was my very first."

"Clara, this is just a preview of the kinds of places and activities in store for us."

"Do you have some specifics you can give me?"

"No, but we'll certainly have more of these love-in marathons, that's for sure. I hope Marcia will agree to a quick divorce. The sooner, the better, so we can get on with our future."

"I think it will be quick, Ben," Clara said.

"Your plan to isolate her from us was a bit harsh, though, don't you think?"

"Yes," Clara replied, "but it was necessary. Otherwise Marcia would be clinging to you from now on."

"I hope she won't be totally devastated," Ben said.

Changing the subject away from Marcia, Clara asked, "What kind of future do you envision for us, Ben?"

"Hopefully we can get married within the next four or five months. Have you given much thought to wedding plans?"

"Perhaps a small church wedding."

"Our wedding will give me an excuse to meet your mom and dad," Ben said happily.

Clara took a deep breath, then said, "Yes, that will be good."

Ben continued, "We need to decide some other things, When would you want to start a family?"

Clara almost choked up, then recovered and lied smoothly, "Maybe after a couple of years."

Ben smiled, then frowned a little. "I still think your treatment of Marcia went too far. She will surely be devastated. I hope I'm not seeing another side of you."

CHAPTER THIRTY-THREE

The next morning both Jeff and Marcia woke early after a good night's sleep.

Jeff asked, "What are your plans when you return?"

"My plans are specific: a quick divorce, time to reflect, and a name change back to Marcia Leed. That name goes back a long way, with a long and proud history, and I want to bring it honor."

"What about Ben and Clara?"

"I'm not a vindictive person. I don't wish them bad luck, but I do have certain vibes, a premonition if you will, like someone is talking to me, saying happiness is not in their future."

"And us?"

"Jeff, you're a great guy. I like you. I'm sure someday our paths will cross again. Call it Karma. Where it will lead, I don't know."

The End

www.ingramcontent.com/pod-product-compliance
Lightning Source LLC
Chambersburg PA
CBHW060329260626
47160CB00007B/2741